CARROLL & GRAF

Adam & Eve

Adam & Eve

Marcus van Heller

Carroll & Graf Publishers, Inc.
New York

First Carroll & Graf edition 1985

Carroll & Graf Publishers, Inc.
260 Fifth Avenue
New York, NY 10001

ISBN: 0-88184-185-4

Manufactured in the United States of America

Adam & Eve

CHAPTER ONE

The lawyer sat on his desk, gently swinging one leg. He spoke in a slow American drawl, with no trace left of an Italian accent, measuring his words, carrying in them the weight of a weary, resigned philosophy...

"There are times when you want to spread an alarm, but nothing has happened. I knew, I knew then and there—I could have finished the whole story that afternoon..." His voice droned on relentlessly... "It wasn't as though there was a mystery to unravel. I could see every step coming, step after step, like a dark figure walking down a hall toward a certain door..." The voice went on speaking out into the dark auditorium from its spotlit aura on the stage. It was dead quiet in the theatre. You would have heard a piece of confetti drop.

Sitting right up in the gallery, which they called the dress circle though it was really only a backward extension of it, the girl sat hunched forward with her arms on the gold-painted handrail. Her buttocks ached a little from sitting for so long on the thin velvet of the seat without moving, but she kept absolutely still so as not to miss a word, the least nuance. The lights went out on Alfieri, the lawyer, and rose on the Sicilian slum apartment near Brooklyn Bridge with Beatrice and

Catherine clearing the table. The girl reached down into her lap with a long, slender, well manicured hand and drew the little pair of opera glasses up to her eyes. She trained them on Beatrice. This was her goddess, Lady Celia Duncan, the finest actress in Britain. She moved them over the girl, Catherine, otherwise Greta Plowman, who was good, very good but not in quite the same category, and so on to Eddie Carbone, Sir George Duncan, the other half of the husband and wife team. He was superb. He gave her a little, sharp thrill in her stomach just to listen to his voice. But it was with Celia Duncan that she identified herself. She could not, after all, change her sex, but she could have Celia Duncan's place one day.

The voices came up to her from the stage, Eddie's, Beatrice's, Catherine's Rodolpho's, Marco's and she absorbed them with her whole being, living their glories with them, feeling their occasional flatness, while the gripping story of consuming possessive passion unfolded itself with the unyielding quality of Greek tragedy. She was aware of nothing else, nobody else at all in the dark theatre around her which now breathed and rustled sometimes, like an animal twitching in its sleep.

She kept the opera glasses clamped to her eyes, ranging them from one to another, her own face tightening in sympathy with theirs, smiling with theirs, frowning with theirs, her breathing faster with theirs, slower with theirs. She watched, her entrails twisted tight like a wrung-out sheet while Marco raised the chair, straining smoothly above his head, and looked down at Eddie with that glint of menace. And she went on staring as the curtain fell and then the safety curtain followed it down and the lights went up all around.

"I can see those adverts without a magnifying glass."

The girl sighed, smiled and turned to her companion.

"Aren't they wonderful," she said.

"They're pretty hot."

He was a handsome boy of about nineteen, a year older than her. He wore a turtle-necked sweater and a pair of smart, tight, Italian trousers. His long, thin face with its rather prominent nose over finely delineated lips carried with it a suggestion of superiority over men of more common clay. His long, dark eyes, which at first glance looked liquid and soft, deepened into a hint of ruthlessness the longer you looked at them.

"Let's have a drink," he said.

"Can we afford it?"

"Of course not. Let's go."

"Just a minute, Adam."

The girl looked around the theatre with a smile of sheer pleasure. It was crowded with people, many now pushing along the aisles towards the bars. It had an air of opulence about its red and gilt and, from the flamboyant gold carving around the boxes and the magnificent cascading chandelier, you could have imagined yourself back in the days of Nell Gwynne and a rowdier audience. The girl could just see the front rows of the stalls, the fur coats and jewellery; all those fat women doing the right social thing, only just heard of Arthur Miller because even they could hardly have missed the name.

She stood up and began to edge along the aisle, followed by the boy. Her name was Eve Patten. It was rather odd that their names should be Adam and Eve and, although they laughed about it, they were both rather embarrassed when people found out and made jokes. She was a secretary, and a very efficient one, in a provincial town in the middle of the south of England. She was a secretary to everyone else, but to herself she was a great actress. Even though amateur productions had been her only outlet so far, she was a great actress. There was really no other point to her life, so that if in appearance she never became one, she was just nothing else in her own mind. She was like the writer who carries the developing book around in his mind year after year after year, going through the motions of jobs, social contacts, empty conversations, but never being anything else but a writer, even though he might never write the book. But all she needed, like everyone, was a start. For this she had not only enthusiasm, a certain amount of talent, but beauty as well. She had been the beauty queen of her city two years running since she left school. "You ought to be in films with your looks," people told her, and that had strengthened her belief that there was a great public waiting for a great actress. She was tall, almost as tall as her companion, with a well developed body and eye-catching legs. Her hair was the colour of champagne, her blue eyes had a slightly luminous quality like the sun on a very blue sea; and her delicate, youthful skin was firmly set over fine bones which had a trace of the oriental in their small, hard prominence.

She was smartly, fashionably dressed; indeed both she and her companion might easily have been taken for two smart young aristocrats from Mayfair.

The bar was crowded, but Adam pushed his way through leaving the girl studying the programme near the door, the focus of attention for several pairs of male eyes who undressed her systematically, imagined that body warmly cushioning theirs in a bed to match her own elegance.

She exhausted the programme and let the images of the play flood back into her head. "A View from the Bridge" was one of the most moving plays she'd seen for some time, although she and Adam had been making this trip to London at weekends for more than a year. Oh for a chance to get in! She thought of Mr. Grampion, the one theatrical agent who hadn't told her: "Not a hope, Miss, all the theatres are booked for a year or more, all the casts set; and in any case looks aren't enough these days, you've got to have talent, experience, masses of experience, and the right moment to help you." Mr. Grampion had said instead: "I might be able to do something for you, but you'll have to sleep with me first." Just like that. No frills, no beating about the bush. They weren't necessary. The market was all his. Mr. Grampion was middle-aged and ugly. The thought would have horrified her even if she hadn't been a virgin. But that had been months and months ago and now she was used to the repeated offer as she made the weary regular round, and nothing else, absolutely nothing, had come up. But she was still frightened. She couldn't even allow herself to start to picture the actual event: the room, the bed, the getting undressed, the seeing him undressed, the contact between the sheets, the... Ugh!

The back of Adam's head came into her conscious thoughts as he leaned over the bar, taking up the glasses. With Adam it could happen. Oh, she had nothing against it, but real opportunities were rare and also something told her, some instinctive sixth sense, that his attitude would change towards her immediately their relationship changed in that way. They'd got very close to it, of course, foolish though she knew it was to play with fire and hope not to get burnt. But always she read something in his eyes, something in that ruthlessness that was suddenly there so naked that she wondered why she didn't see it all the time. And that pulled her up. It wasn't any corny woman magazine trash about

"They don't respect you once they've had you," it was just a particular understanding of an individual character —and she knew her Adam. Because he was very much like her.

He came weaving back towards her, a bottle of tonic and a gin in one hand, a glass of brown ale in the other. She smiled and raised an eyebrow.

"A beer would have done, Adam. We won't have the fare to get to Aunt Beatie's if you throw it around like that."

He grinned.

"I won a sweepstake at the office," he said. "Shilling in, twenty out—have another."

Adam worked for the biggest firm of solicitors in their town. He was one of the clerks. Both he and Eve were misfits, which was almost certainly why they kept each other's company. Adam was a fine painter, at least a lot of local people thought he was a fine painter, including Mr. Grant, his art master at school and now his tutor at the evening classes to which he went for the sake of the cheaper paint and canvases. But if it was difficult to get on the stage, it was even more difficult to get an exhibition. Local ones weren't worth having and London—well. While she made the round of the agents, Adam made the round of the galleries, pleading, cajoling, looking at the work on view, frequently wondering exactly what it had that his hadn't. Like Eve, he had one overwhelming disadvantage. He didn't know anyone. Not one of the right people. Not even one of the off-right people. Not a soul who mattered, except for his art master who, in spite of a more cosmopolitan history, had for years been buried away in the provincial town which was now his whole, quiet life.

The couple stood in the bar, sipping their drinks, talking about the play. Adam was particularly impressed with the scenery, which combined two views in one by which you could see the interior of the apartment on the left hand and the dockside, simply and vividly evoked with a black silhouette of scaffolding, on the right.

"As a matter of fact, I wouldn't mind doing a bit of stage designing," he said. "But it's not worth much, unless you have a big name."

The bell went for the second act. The interval was, as usual, much too short to enable you to have a drink in comfort. They tipped back their glasses and pushed back up the stairs to the dress-circle-cum-gallery, with the lights already going dim.

During the second act the girl sat breathless on the edge of her not very comfortable seat, letting the play swamp her, the words subdue her to a state of trance... Alfieri: "You won't have a friend in the world, Eddie! Even those who understand you will turn against you..." Catherine: "I'm gonna get married, Eddie. So if you wanna come, the wedding be on Saturday... " Beatrice: "She loves him, Eddie. Why don't you give her a good word?"... the Immigration Officers... the seizure of the illegal immigrants... the fight... Eddie's death. And Alfieri at the end: "Most of the time we settle for half and I like it better. But the truth is holy, and even as I know how wrong he was, and his death useless, I tremble, for I confess that something perversely pure calls to me from his memory—not purely good—but himself purely..." She repeated to herself in her mind the words which seemed to have meaning for her... "not purely good, but himself purely." The curtain came down. These was a long moment's pause and then a rapture of applause. The applause thrilled her like blood coursing through her veins, setting all her flesh a-tingle, making her head suddenly hot. She pictured the applause as being for herself, saw her own figure on the brightly lit stage as Lady Celia and Sir George joined hands and moved forward together away from the rest of the cast to a sudden increase in the volume of applause. And then Lady Celia drew back and Sir George stepped forward a couple of paces alone to another lift in the acclamation. Eve clapped until her hands stung. Of course it should be the other way round to please her, with Lady Celia alone on the stage, but of course Eddie Carbone was the major character in the play. The curtain fell, rose, fell and rose again until finally it came down with that air of finality which quelled even the most ardent fans. The clapping petered out and the audience was making for the exits, a swell of animated chatter and shuffling feet rising through the auditorium like hot air.

Eve glanced at Adam and they stood up and began to move towards the steps of the aisle. She looked at the people, tightly packed, brushing their way out, but without seeing them. She had made a decision. It was the last sight of Eddie dying in the arms of Beatrice. It had called to her like a saint, or a devil, calling to men to follow him. She needed to be on that stage. It was more than life, more than disgust for Mr. Grampion. She would sleep with him and he would get her a part. That was how the beginning would be. And then if necessary she would sleep with him again or with anyone else who could push her on. She glanced back at Adam's handsome face and he looked at her quizzically. She would have liked it to be Adam, the first time. But one had to work these things out or one never got anywhere. She thought of all the girls back at the office, their total lack of ambition, except to own a house or a vacuum sweeper and to keep their boyfriends so that they married them with the biggest show of wedding they could manage, together with spotty, featureless photographs in the local papers. Not one of them used any real charm to get a more interesting life. She sometimes wondered if they thought of their boyfriends in any different way from their dream of a refrigerator. And sometimes, when one of them slept with the boy, giving way to pressure, how surprised she was when his ardour cooled. It was a game, after all, and you had to play it.

CHAPTER TWO

Eve hated the long, long tube journey out to her aunt's house in the suburbs. It was one of those typically semi-detached doll's houses with tiny rooms and a neat garden, three up and two down as regards the rooms. Everything was spotless, for her aunt cleaned and cleaned until you were almost afraid to put one foot in front of another in case you stepped on something you shouldn't or knocked something over. The area was the sort that working class people strove for when they wanted to better themselves, neat, green, uniform, fairly "good" and characterless as a tailor's dummy. Her aunt had devoted her whole life to getting it, dragging her husband along with her. Everything else had been sacrificed; no effort to develop taste, brain, enjoyment of life, nothing. Now her aunt suffered from the enormous sense of inadequacy, lightly covered with a veneer of snobbery, which all such people who have made material betterment their god are prey to.

Eve knew that her aunt regarded her with a mixture of adoration and disapproval. Adoration for her appearance and general presence, which blinded people to her origins, adoration too for her ambition and determination to succeed. Disapproval of her desire to succeed in such an uncertain, unknown, weird world as that of the stage rather than stick at her good job in the office. She didn't really approve of Adam either. She didn't understand what he was talking about most of the time and she felt, quite correctly, that he disliked her and looked down on her values.

"If I lived in London, I wouldn't dream of living out so far," she said, as the train swayed through the dark tunnel. "Might just as well live at home."

"Doesn't make any difference to your aunt," Adam said. "The metropolis hasn't got anything to offer her. She doesn't want theatre, restaurants, art galleries, museums, the colour of people. As long as she can make an occasional trip in to the sales so that she can imagine she's getting something for next to nothing, she's happy."

"You sound like the appreciative guest should," Eve said.

"You know I'd just as soon sleep on the Embankment."

Eve shivered.

"Give me a warm bed every time," she said. "Even if it does mean playing the hypocrite to get it."

The train thundered on and they fell into silence. She glanced slyly at his face. Their relationship had rather peculiar ups and downs, due to her refusal to sleep with him. Now was one of the downs when they were sort of polite and he sounded cynical and bitter. Tomorrow, or in an hour, it would be quite different.

Her thoughts went back to the last tender episode. After dusk in a field on the outskirts of the town. Her heart missed a beat at the thought of it. They had lain in the dark shadow of a bus and she'd been able to feel in his pants the hard bulge which confessed his desire. Their kissing had reached a level of extreme sexuality, to the point where it no longer compensated for the real thing. She remembered his hand on her breasts, over the brassiere, the way she'd made no attempt to stop him undoing the catch, thinking that would be all right, the tender tingling of his fingers over the hot, bare flesh of her breast, the way he pinched her nipple suddenly, making her squeal and pant so that she hadn't stopped his hand as it stole up her leg with one smooth, unhesitating movement and went straight under the thin strip of her briefs to the moist lips of her vagina. Her mouth went dry now to think of how near they'd come. She'd been almost beside herself as he massaged her clitoris and reached his fingers deep into the hot passage between her legs. He'd tried to take off her briefs, the night air had been cold on her completely bared thighs. But she'd made a huge effort and stopped him. They'd argued, threatened, pleaded and finally he'd got up in disgust and lit a cigarette. They'd both sat smoking silently in the darkness. She pretending she was merely frightened, rather than admit that she wouldn't risk losing him. He bitterly reproaching her, showing her the packet of Durex, which would make it safe. She had said nothing was 100 per cent safe. So they had remained with their passions cooling and the uncomfortable wetness between her legs growing colder and colder, until bad temper had worn itself out and he'd seen her home and left. He hadn't yet recovered from that refusal.

She stole another glance at his handsome, slightly bitter profile. What a handsome couple we make, she suddenly thought.

They reached the distant suburb and caught the last bus for the short journey to her aunt's house. Everything was in darkness. All these joyless people had gone to bed ages ago, to bed from one day which was just like the next. Everything they did was just like the thing they'd done before and would do again next time. I wouldn't be my aunt for ten thousand pounds, she thought—a hundred thousand.

Aunt Beatie let them in, kissed her, shook hands with Adam. She was pleased and nervous, as she always was when she had to organise anything, such as a late supper for two people. She pottered about the kitchen while they made themselves at home. Uncle Den had gone to bed.

"How was the play, dear?

"Wonderful, auntie."

"What did you say it was?"

"*A View from the Bridge*—Arthur Miller."

"Arthur Miller. Oh yes, dear, that would be good. He's been on television. I forget what it was called—all about a commercial traveller who treated his wife badly."

Eve sighed and Adam grinned at her maliciously.

The aunt asked no more questions about the play. She'd made all the conversation on that subject of which she was capable. While she prepared their rather unimaginative cold salad with cups of tea, she talked about the sales and what she'd bought—all useless things she'd wear once and never again. She also talked about some of her friends whom Adam and Eve hardly knew and she talked about the weather. She would have liked to mention something harmless about the Aldermaston March, whose stupidity, as she thought it, fascinated her in some perverse way. But she was vaguely afraid there might be some subtlety about it and its motives that she didn't understand and either

Adam or Eve—particularly Adam—might make her feel an utter imbecile with her ignorance. She was, of course, after starting out as a Socialist and getting where she had with the help of Socialism, an out and out Tory. One of those Tories who knows nothing about Europe, Africa, the H-Bomb, housing policies, exports and imports or anything like that. But who feels in her bones that the Socialists might take her refrigerator away and give it to a slum family, or build a road across her back garden without a by-your-leave, one of those, in fact, who sees about three inches high.

Eve washed up afterwards to show willing, and the aunt indicated their beds—clean sheets, everything clinical. Eve in the back bedroom, Adam in the box-room. They all said goodnight.

Eve undressed slowly, studying herself in the mirror. No superfluous flesh, creamy smooth skin, taut, high breasts and gentle, sloped shoulders. She mouthed a few lines from the play, bringing tears to her eyes with her silent passion. She didn't put on her pyjamas. Instead she pulled back the curtains and looked out into the neat, tidy, moonlit garden. Oh for a blade of grass out of place, she thought. Why doesn't aunt realise this garden and this house don't reflect life at all and that's what makes them so artificial. But then, aunt didn't realise her life was artificial either, so how could she? She thought of Mr. Grampion. It was to him her thoughts kept coming, even though she tried to think of other things. She smoothed her hands over her body and shuddered. Even though the thought of him doing that had no reality, she shuddered. She sat on the clean coverlet of the bed and looked down at the soft, silky hair at the V of her loins. To imagine him putting his thing up inside there was just impossible. She went suddenly hot—a strange mixture of revulsion and desire.

Her door opened gently and she swung round. Adam slid into the moonlit room, wearing only his tight, Y-front pants.

"Adam!" she hissed. "You must be mad!"

He came over towards her with his slim, muscular body which the moon turned silver, and the heavy sag in the front of his pants and the big protuberance pointing at her through the cloth.

"Adam," she said again with soft intensity. "Auntie'll hear you. You mustn't stay."

But he came at her and pulled her up into his arms, naked as she was and kissed her with fury, splaying her lips out so that she automatically splurged her tongue into his mouth. She felt frightened and hollow in the pit of her stomach and she fell back under his pressure so that they were both stretched out on top of the bed. His hands began to rake her body, smoothing over the swell of the breasts. He bit her nipple and she checked with difficulty the cry that came into her throat.

"No Adam, no!" she whispered furiously, scenting the danger.

But his hand roamed at large, over ribs and belly, stroked the soft pubic hair so that she itched between her legs and squirmed away. But his hand came after her and splayed the lips of her vagina apart as his lips had hers. She gasped, unable to choke the sound. She squirmed on his fingers.

"Adam, Adam," she whispered into his face, "this is madness. Not here, not here!"

He slipped out of his pants. She heard him grunt at his own nakedness. She felt the huge, hot throbbing of his penis against her hip. His fingers raped her passage, delving deeper and deeper. Her neck arched and she moved her face from side to side, gritting her teeth with the word "No" concertina-ing in her head.

Adam took her hand and placed it on his prick. She let it rest there. It was enormous. She'd never have realised they were so big. Instinctively she began to stroke it and then to massage it, rubbing the skin back and forth. She remembered what a fast friend of hers had once told her and felt down for his balls. Their hairiness and texture surprised her. She'd heard how vulnerable they were and stroked them gently, holding them in her palm. Adam was grinding his teeth and grunting between breaths. She felt a light moisture cold on her thigh. She wondered if he'd come, but his prick was still as stiff as a ramrod. That must be the lubricant they talked about.

"Eve, Eve—I want you, I must, must, must...!" he whispered frenziedly.

"No Adam, no!"

She must let him, she told herself through her longing. But she couldn't stop him if he really tried. She was losing the fight with herself.

"Eve, Eve!"

He rolled on top of her suddenly.

"No Adam, no."

She jacknifed her legs down and felt his penis caught, hard and long between her thighs. She pressed her thighs together. Adam moaned and and panted, fighting to lift his penis up and into her quim. She resisted desperately, feeling his prick coming nearer, jerking and thrusting between her legs.

Suddenly Adam let out a hoarse cry. She felt his prick expand and contract against the sensitive flesh of her thighs. He gasped and gasped and gasped again. She felt hot fluid running all over her thighs, dripping down between them.

Adam collapsed on her body, panting, almost sobbing.

She stroked his head. My god, she thought, what a racket. And as if prompted by her thought, there was movement on the landing outside and her aunt's voice cried out anxiously.

"Are you all right, dear?"

Eve went rigid.

"Quick, under the bed in case she comes in," she whispered.

Adam slid reluctantly off her and disappeared.

Eve tried to still her heavy breathing and called out.

"I'm all right, aunty, what's up?"

"I thought I heard you call out?"

"Just a cough, aunt."

"Would you like some cough mixture, dear? There's some in the bathroom. Shall I get it for you?"

"No, no, aunty. It's nothing at all. Just got something in my throat. I'm all right, really."

All right then, dear. Goodnight."

"Goodnight."

Eve waited until she heard her aunt's door close and then she got off the bed and switched on the light. Adam was lying on the rug. He looked exhausted and hadn't bothered to hide under the bed. In any case, he'd left his pants on the coverlet and, worse than that, there was a great trail of heavy, glue-coloured sperm all across the clean, peach coverlet.

Eve pushed back her hair from her face. All her nerves were a-jangle. She went to Adam and caught his shoulder. He kneeled up and she pulled him to her and kissed him. They held each other for a minute or two.

"We'd better clean up," she whispered then.

She slipped out of his arms, found her handkerchief and wiped her legs. She began to wipe the coverlet, but, although the sperm came off, it left a thick, greasy mark which was clearly going to show.

"Good god," she said. "Aunt will never get over this."

"It's all right," Adam said, behind her. "She'll never guess in a million years what it is."

She looked round at his sardonically grinning face. She looked at the whole of him, standing there in the full light with his deflated penis dripping moisture down onto her aunt's clean rug. She grinned back and began to laugh. They both began to laugh. It became almost uncontrollable. She could tell now that this was one of the ups.

CHAPTER THREE

Eve saw Adam off at Waterloo the next morning. He had to go back to their home town because his art master particularly wanted him to meet some old friend who had some influence in the art world and might be able to help him. Mr. Grant had been rather vague about the person, but very insistent on them meeting. No chance of help could ever be turned down.

Eve, in the meantime, would continue to see agents in the hope of getting something. This, at least was her story.

They kissed *au revoir* on the train steps in the great, dim cavern of the station, with steam gushing and whistles blowing and people scurrying to and fro shouting their farewells, calling for porters.

"I wish I didn't have to go back," Adam said. "Perhaps we could finish what we started."

"I thought we did," Eve said. "Anyway we certainly finished Aunt Beatie's coverlet. It was stiff as a board this morning. I made the bed and left it. Perhaps she'll think I had a celestial visitation."

"She'll be envious," Adam said.

The whistle blew, the green flag was waved, the last door slammed and the train strained slowly away out of the station. Eve went back through the barrier and caught a bus over Waterloo Bridge to the West End.

In a little street in Soho, near the film offices, she walked past a narrow doorway with a bronze tablet at its side. The tablet said: J. Grampion Ltd., Theatrical Agent. Eve walked past the doorway half a dozen times. Finally she went into a bar, ignoring the stares of the clientele, bought herself a gin with her meagre resources, knocked it back straight and went out again without looking at anyone. The liquor warmed her inside. It didn't amount to much, but it was a help.

She went up the stairs from the doorway. There was no carpet, they were covered with rubber pads. At the top of the stairs was a landing, dark and gloomy, and half way along a sign hanging over a door said "Enquiries." She went along to the door, stood still outside for twenty seconds fighting to control her breath, her fast-beating heart, and then went in.

An automatic bell jangled and the well-known secretary looked up from her typewriter. She was a supercilious young woman, rather plain, but making the best of herself. She had extraordinarily large breasts. Eve had sometimes wondered how many inches over 40 they were. She had also wondered if, to keep her job, she had to lie on her back for Mr. Grampion once in a while. With breasts like that, she could be able to keep him at arm's length in emergency.

The secretary raised her eyebrows and said in an ultra-refined voice, whose vowel sounds you'd never find in a dictionary: "Mr. Grampion's rawthah busy. Caaan you wait?"

"All right," Eve said.

The girl motioned her to the familiar and admittedly comfortable leather chair. She made no effort to communicate with her employer, which irritated Eve, feeling as she did that the waiting was as often due to the secretary's whim as to Grampion's pressure of work.

After about five minutes the secretary picked up a phone extension and said into it.

"Miss Patten to see you, Mr. Grampion. Are you busy or shall I tell her to come in?"

She listened, replaced the receiver and resumed her typing without looking at Eve. Eve sighed. There was no point in getting hot under the collar when you wanted something. This she knew from bitter experience. You had to wait until the power was in your own hands.

After another five minutes, the secretary looked up as if she was surprised to see the client still patiently waiting.

"Mr. Grampion will see you now," she said.

"Thaaank you so much," Eve said, unable to resist the mimicry.

The secretary looked at her sharply and Eve knocked on the frosted glass of the inner door and went in.

John Grampion was sitting behind a broad, baize-topped table, making a few notes with a handsome pen. There was always an air of make-believe about his work. He was a fat, heavy man of about 50 with fish eyes that looked as if they couldn't stand to hear another word from you. He had a small, slightly turned up nose and thin, hard lips over a full, fleshy chin. He dressed well and spoke well, but with a certain rather coarse suaveness which theatrical agents are either born with or acquire. His office was sumptuous compared with the secretary's. It was fitted with a dove-grey carpet and decorated in white and grey with small touches of blue. There were a couple of elegant modern chairs and an elegant modern sideboard along a wall. The other wall was a window which looked out, rather surprisingly, on a charming little courtyard.

"Well, well, Miss Patten. How are you?" he asked, looking at her with eyes which were devoid of any generosity but chock-full of sensuality and lust.

"I'm fine, Mr. Grampion, thank you. I just came to see if you have anything you can throw my way."

Grampion drew out a card index from a small cabinet perched on one side of his desk. He flicked through the card index till he found her name. On the card he had a few details about her. They were not very encouraging. No experience to speak of at all. Also scrawled on the card in pencil were the words "Might eventually" which referred to matters other than theatrical.

He turned to a similar cabinet on the other side of his desk and made a show of looking through another card index. He closed the cabinet and looked up.

"Nothing suitable, I'm afraid, Miss Patten," he said, staring insolently at her legs.

Eve had sat at his invitation on one of the chairs opposite the desk. As he looked at her legs she deliberately hitched up her skirt half an inch. She didn't know how to broach the subject.

Grampion raised his eyes slowly up her legs and body to her face and gave her a long searching look.

"Let me see, when did you last come?" he asked.

"About a month ago," she said.

"And on that occasion I had nothing."

"I don't know. Only on certain conditions."

Grampion smiled lewdly. He wasn't the slightest embarrassed. He was enjoying himself, sensing that he had fresh prey.

"And have you changed you mind, by any chance?"

Eve hesitated. It was still not too late to refuse. She

blushed slowly.

"Yes," she said, looking at his desk.

"Well, well. How very, very nice."

Grampion rose from the desk. There was real lustful delight in his fish eyes. He could hardly take in yet that this beautiful chicken had finally come to roost in his nest. He was very tired of Miss Jones, his secretary, in spite of those enormous mouthfuls of breast of hers and it was some time since he'd had an offer such as this. He went to the sideboard and opened it.

"Let's have a drink, my dear. Your name is Eve, I understand, and mine is John. What will you have?"

Eve fought back her truculence. Might as well make it all as easy as possible. She wondered where he wanted to do it. On the fitted carpet? Not with his secretary next door and this big window, surely.

"I'll have a gin and tonic," she said. "A double gin."

"A triple, by all means, if you'd like it," Grampion said, smiling delightedly. "A little more than you fancy does you good, I always say."

He poured an enormous gin and added a little tonic. He poured a large Scotch for himself, added a drop of water and walked across to Eve. He handed her the drink and stood looking down at her. He made no attempt to touch her.

"Chin-chin," he said.

Eve didn't answer. She took a long, deep, spine-tingling swig of the drink. It seared through her, easing her tensions almost immediately. What did it matter? she asked herself. What did it matter? You ate things you didn't like. Visited places you didn't like. Put up with cuts and sores. Nothing was really unbearable any more than anyone was indispensable.

Grampion's eyes ranged over her, gloating over her body. He licked his thin lips and touched her neck with his fingers. She sat stockstill, looking at her drink. He took his fingers away and said: "Well, my dear Eve. I shall be through in half an hour. I suggest you go and have a coffee at the Expresso two corners up. Have anything you like there. I'll pick you up there in half an hour."

"What about a part?" she said. "What can you do for me?"

He smiled smoothly.

"Well, as always in this profession, there are certain changes that can be made in the recommendations," he said. "There's this new play coming on at the Criterion in two months' time. I've already suggested someone for one of the parts that I think you could fill just as well. It's not the lead, of course. Can't expect that straight away. But it's a meaty small part with good lines, good entrances, good exits—a chance to make a real impression if you grab it. I'll start to work on it right away."

"What's the play?" she asked.

"It's this new one by William Inge. He's fed up with New York. Told me so himself when I was over there a little while ago. Wants to try London. I can give you full details later and of the part. Leave everything to me."

Eve left his office and walked past the secretary, who glanced at her suspiciously.

"Don't bother to show me out," Eve said. "I can tell by the look of you how overworked and underpaid you are, poor thing."

The secretary's mouth sagged and Eve closed the door behind her with a grim little smile and went down the stairs to find the coffee bar. She hoped they had plenty of delicious and expensive sandwiches to put on Grampion's account.

CHAPTER FOUR

Eve leaned back in the big Oldsmobile. Trust him to have a big, flashy American car. But at least he wasn't mean with his money once he'd got what he wanted. She'd made a pig of herself over the sandwiches at the coffee bar but he hadn't batted an eyelid at the bill and had promptly whisked her off to an elegant bar for drinks. He was in the best of spirits. He was even faintly amusing. If only he hadn't been such a greasy character and had such greasy looks, she would have found the thought of the forthcoming ordeal easier to bear.

Now they were flashing out to his flat at Maida Vale. The area where the expensive prostitutes lived. She felt quite high, but instead of making her gay it had depressed her.

Grampion chattered: gossip, theatrical gossip all the time, dropping names, spending money in words like water. She found herself wondering if he really knew all these people as well as he pretended, or did he get it all from the newspaper and cinema magazine diaries.

They raced up the Edgeware Road, beating the lights at every hundred yards until they came to the smooth stretch of sumptuous flats which heralded the golden mile of Maida Vale. Here Grampion turned off with a screech of brakes, shot up a side street, down another, as if he couldn't wait to get his pants off and pulled up in front of a small block of stone and brick flats with big glass doors leading into quite an elegant hall.

Grampion parked the car and led her in. It was clear that he made more money than his office indicated. They went up in the lift, cramped together. But although he gloated over her, he still didn't touch her, as if he were savouring the moment to come, not prepared to spoil it with preliminaries which might be abortive.

On the third floor they got out and walked along the carpeted passage to a door at the end of it. Grampion let them in with a key and Eve walked into what was virtually a one-room flat. One room, elegant and comfortable, in which Grampion slept on a divan at night, lazed on it during the day. Off the tiny entrance which led into this room were a tiny kitchen and a rather larger bathroom. It was all shining and clean, obviously serviced.

"A small place but mine own," Grampion said. "Very expensive, very useful and convenient. Take off your coat."

She took off her coat obediently and he took it and hung it in a concealed cupboard in the entrance hall. He looked at her in her elegant tight-fitting black dress which showed off her champagne coloured hair and blue eyes so well. He licked his lips and the delight had gone out of his eyes leaving only an urgent lust which made his whole face even uglier.

Eve walked before him right into the little room. He came up behind her and put his hand on her buttocks. She stopped.

"Beautiful," he murmured. "You are beautiful." He ran his hand over her bottom and then up over her breasts, still standing behind her. She could hear the wheeze of his breathing. She felt nothing at all. And then he moved away again and said: "Well, let's have one for the bed, as you might say."

She shuddered then, a little shiver of revulsion which started at her toes and ran right up to her scalp. It would be on that divan. There was no mystery any longer. No sheltering vagueness. It would be there that he would do things to her, with his grossness and his ugliness. She looked out of the small window to the front courtyard as if to escape into the sun and the fresh air. When she turned back, he had brim-full glasses of drink and was holding one out to her.

"You certainly like your liquor," she said, almost disgustedly, though she had no objection to liquor at all.

"It always improves my performance," he said with a leer. "And with such a beautiful girl, I particularly want to be in top form."

He knocked back a large part of the drink and then he began to take off his clothes. Eve watched him, half fascinated, as if his undressing had nothing to do with her at all.

"Shall I do it for you?" he asked, looking at her dress.

"I can manage very well, thank you," she said.

She undid the buttons of her dress at the back, wriggled it off her shoulders, down over her hips and stepped out of it. She felt Grampion's eyes devouring her but she didn't look at him. She pulled her slip over her head, picked up both garments and draped them over a chair. She felt suddenly extremely naked. She also felt a little dizzy from the drink. She glanced at Grampion. He was naked, taking off his socks. His body was as huge and gross as his face; his yellow flesh sagged and perspired so that she could see it glistening across the room. His penis jutted out under the overhang of his belly, surrounded by a jet black fuzz of hair. It reminded her of a cannon poking from a thicket under an overhanging cliff. She giggled hysterically and then shuddered violently. The thought of his fat body on hers revolted her. The thought...! She couldn't go through with it. She felt quite clearly now to the depths of her being that she couldn't go through with it.

Grampion had stood up and turned towards her. His mouth was open, his fish eyes popped, he gazed wildly at her long legs in the sheer nylon stoockings, the stretch of chalk white thigh above, the pert breasts which made smooth hillocks, above the cup-shaped brassiere, the chalk white midriff, the long strength of the hips. His look appalled her and she said, gasping: "I made a mistake, Mr. Grampion. I can't do it!"

"But my dear—your part."

He came towards her. His eyes held no humanity—lust, cruel and unyielding, shone in them like an unforgiving headlight which permitted no shelter.

"Your future... your future...," he murmured. And his body towered over her, his fish eyes shone into her face, absorbing it.

"No, no, Mr. Grampion. I mean it. I can't do it. I'm leaving now. It doesn't matter about the part. I don't want it."

His arms enveloped her and his face covered her and his lips engulfed her, wetly, voraciously, sucking her own mouth into his like a vacuum cleaner. She began to struggle. She was so dizzy she could hardly stand up, kept feeling she was falling. He held her tight. She couldn't tell whether he was so strong or she was so weak. His tongue was in her mouth like a great wet fish, exploring, brushing wetly all around the inside. She was overwhelmed with his smell of sweat and perfume, and his great amorphous body flowed around her, bulging here, receding there, inescapable.

"No, no, no," she insisted. "Let me go. How dare you!"

She struggled furiously but he moved her with him across the room as if they were one body, seeming to flow with her struggles so that she seemed to have nothing definite to fight against. She felt a great, frenzied fear in her belly and her body and limbs began to tremble uncontrollably. Te dizziness was worse, the room was going round.

She found she was parallel with the ceiling. It couldn't be true. The ceiling was coming down to meet her and the fish eyes joined it, like spotlights coming at her in a dark theatre. She struggled vaguely, turned her face away. There was a great weight on her and her clothes were being removed as if by some inevitable, mechanical process... And the great, crushing amorphous body was emitting all sorts of noises which fused together in a great thunder which seemed to split her eardrums until she was sure that it was in fact the ceiling that was crashing down on her head; and then, between her legs, whose existence she'd forgotten, there was a sudden deep, thrusting entry as if a red-hot pole had been shoved into her body. She screamed and jerked away, but it followed her and the mouth came back on hers, eating at her lips and her tongue and the red-hot poker came in and in, drubbing into her cunt so that it seemed on fire and her whole lower body seemed to be split apart and tears ran down her cheeks and she began to sob and the room went round and round and finally she passed right out.

Eve came to, much later. She wasn't sure how much later, but it was beginning to get dark. She was aware that her breasts were being stroked and that there was a great hot weight of flesh along her back. She was lying on her side. She was on a divan with a blanket over her. She was naked except for her torn stockings. She was in a strange room. Her head was aching. Her vagina was aching—and sore—and it felt as if a solid block of something was inside it, but there was nothing. Gradually it began to come back to her. Without stirring she dropped her eyes to the fat, fleshy hand which moved over her breasts, disarranging the blanket. It had happened. It was over. She'd had it. She was no longer one of the vast legion of virgins. Well and truly not, by the fury of the inflamed fire between her legs. It didn't seem to matter now. It seemed rather unimportant. All that fear. It was all in the mind before the event, like most things. Except it would have been better for it to have happened with someone she liked, like Adam, instead of this coarse slug. The only thing was to think of the reward: a part. Even that seemed rather remote at the moment, however. She felt terribly thirsty. She spoke to the room ahead of her.

"I'd like a glass of water."

The hand ran down her belly and the fingers traced a line over her hip to rest on the hollow of her buttock. There was a great heaving movement. Grampion slithered off the divan and it rose up an inch or two carrying her up with it.

"Certainly, my dear," his voice said. "For the sake of your tight little fanny you shall have one."

He came into view from the foot of the divan. She watched his plump buttocks shake as he walked to the sideboard. His intimate penetration of her had no reality. It was impossible to believe it.

"A hair of the dog is better," he said.

"I want a long drink. I'm parched."

"Hair of the dog's still better."

She watched him pour a little drop of gin into a tumbler. He took two bottles of tonic, the split size, and drowned the gin with them. He handed her the tumbler and she drank greedily, leaning over the edge of the divan. He climbed over her and lay down behind her again. She ignored his heavy heat, thinking—almost without thinking—how differently one viewed these things once they'd happened.

The tonic was wonderful, braced her and the gin in it warmed her stomach. She felt his body snuggle closer. He had a big erection; she could feel it against the cleavage of her bottom.

"You have smoother skin than any other woman I've known," he said.

"Thanks," she said flatly.

"You're the first virgin I've ever had," he said thoughtfully, as if he were flicking back through a car index, checking that he hadn't made a mistake.

"Thanks again. What makes you think I was?"

"You were wild until you passed out. It was like holy murder."

He said the words with gleeful pleasure. It was clear he'd enjoyed every moment of the assault.

She said nothing. She simply lay there, her mind almost a blank, a blank into whose corners occasionally flickered the thought of her standing on a stage somewhere, the thought of Aunt Beatie and the sperm on the coverlet, of Adam, of her mother and father.

"What time is it?" she asked.

She felt his pulsing rod of flesh press against her buttocks and he placed his hands on her waist, drawing her bottom at his loins.

"Quite early," he said.

"I must be going. I have to go home."

"Plenty of trains," he said. "If not I'll run you down."

She relaxed. That took the pressure off anyway. Might as well get all she could for what she'd given.

His body pressed very close to her and his lips took a nibble from the nape of her neck to her shoulder. She lay still, uncooperative, and felt is hand ooze between her thighs where the buttocks joined them. It no longer shocked her to have him exploring her nudity in this way. It didn't please her either, but it didn't shock her in any way at all. His fingers caressed the lips of her vagina and finally entered and stroked the walls of the passage. She felt a little wet down there and contracted her bowels in spite of herself. She supposed you couldn't help getting a slight kick out of it even if the partner was obnoxious. His rigid penis oozed between her thighs after his fingers and prodded for the opening in her pelvis.

"I'm too sore," she said. "Leave me alone."

"Now, now," he said unctuously, pretending to be only joking, but reminding her of his power, "you want that part, don't you."

Her mind froze and she gritted her teeth in a spasm of anger. He could hold this over her for anything and for ever until she got the part. But the spasm passed.

Now the chunky knob of his prick had found the inflamed ring of moist flesh. She groaned as it moved into her, but he ignored her discomfiture. At the moment of entry, he seemed to lose himself in a torrent of passion. His breath came up from his belly in raking gasps and he skewered furiously and completely into her so that she cried out and tried to pull away.

"You're hurting me!" she gasped.

But he held her fast, with a hand curving round each hip so that the fingers pressed hard into the firm, elastic flesh of her abdomen. He moved into her like a series of ripples of water, growing ever larger. She gasped and squirmed, caught like a stuck pig on the end of a lance. His thighs were hairy and hot along the undersides of hers and the hairs of his loins brushed her behind. He pummelled into her with force. He seemed to fill the whole of her belly, up to her breasts. Sometimes he hurt her in some unaccountable way, with a sudden extra sharp point of pain. At other moments it seemed as if he was exploding in her like gunpowder, spreading wide parts of her that had always been hidden and closed. Behind her in the bed he was like a tempestuous sea, tossing and whirling and thundering and battering against her ass.

"My god," she heard him yell and his fingers dug deeply into her belly, making her squeal. She felt an extra pressure against her hips and his fingers began to pull and guide her over onto her knees, levering himself up behind her. She let herself be led, although she felt extremely undignified and, somehow, completely abased before him as if she were some old-world slave bowing before her master while he took her almost anonymously.

Now he slithered close between her widespread thighs, pushing them apart even more with his knees and he squirmed his prick right up, and deep, up to the very hilt, into her quim. Now that she was spread out he seemed to invade her even deeper, splitting her body in two, forcing gasp after gasp from her panting mouth. Her back began to ache from the pressure of his hands around her waist, bending her waist down so that her rump soared up towards his face. She felt totally naked to her soul. Her loins tingled and clamped, a thousand red hot bars inside battering one against the other, sending out a million sparks throughout her body from the molten nucleus of her vagina. His flesh buffetted her buttocks with bruising force. She heard him give little whining screams. She thought, My god, he's not using anything, but she herself was on fire and unable to complain, only to cough out a gathering storm of passion. He squirmed and skewered, bringing a cry from her throat with every in-thrust. He seemed to be getting bigger and bigger and going higher and higher towards her very throat. Her breasts heaved and danced. She found herself swaying a dance with her behind on the stem of his prick, like some windblown flower. She was sore as hell but afire with a great building pressure, too, a liquid screeching pressure in her loins which was growing to a pinpoint of agony. She couldn't think of anything but the enormous, agonisingly sweet buildup inside her. This was it. This was it. Somehow she'd never thought it would really happen to her. The buildup grew into agreat, expanding bubble which was swelling up her inside to several times its real size. She screamed and screamed again, loud and shrill, and the bubble burst and it seemed like blood rushing from her loins in a torrent, hot and wet, and she screamed again with the tears of fright and ecstasy and relief running down her cheeks.

She began to calm a little. She was trembling all over and her stomach was quaking as if she'd just missed being run over by an express train—and still he was stuffing his penis up into her cunt with fury, wheezing between his teeth and practically hurling her off the divan with every harsh forward thrust. Now her forgotten soreness began to reassert itself. Her vagina felt scoured as if someone had used a potato peeler on its lining. She gritted her teeth, wondering how long she could stand it, and then she heard him muttering to himself, a muttering which grew into a waterfall of moaning, groaning agony, rose to a gasping howl and exploded into a barking shout. She felt nothing in her quim except that his thrusts slowed to great solid, slow heaves and she knew he was coming right up inside her with dangerous, child-giving sperm and she thought, "My god, that's twice today. Suppose I have a child," and then he fell forward on her with a groan and such a mountain of weight that she collapsed under him. He lay on her for some time, gasping, and then she said: "Why didn't you use something. Suppose I have a child?"

"It's all right," he said. "I'm sterile as a clinic. We could do this for years."

After a few minutes more, she protested and he rolled off her. She slithered off the bed and went into the bathroom. She cleaned herself up, spread her hands over her aching loins, put on a dressing gown she found on a hook on the door and went back into the room where he was still lying fat and naked and sated on the divan.

"Tell me about the play and the part," she said. "And then you can drive me home."

She found she did not feel very well disposed towards him. Though it now seemed as if they'd known each other for years.

"The part?"

"Yes, the part in the Inge play?"

"Oh, yes."

He leered at her. "Well it's not absolutely certain the play's going on, of course. Things are very uncertain in the theatre world, you know."

She saw it all in a flash of understanding that hit her like a thunderbolt. But she refused to believe it immediately. It was impossible that, if it was the way it seemed, that it wouldn't have occurred to her before. So it couldn't be. Thus her reasoning went.

"How uncertain?" she asked. "And why didn't you say that before?"

"Can't tell," he said. "Trouble with the managements."

"What's the play called? What's it about?" It seemed incredible to her now that she hadn't asked these simple questions before. Why hadn't she got something in writing? That was elementary.

"I don't remember the name off hand," he said. "It's one of these domestic drama-cum-psychological-tracts, you know."

"Well, what's the part for me?"

"Young wife, doesn't get on well with her husband."

"What's her name?"

She saw him hesitate and he saw her see him. He grinned.

"You ask too many questions," he said. "I told you the play might not go on at all. Wait and see what happens."

She flew at him then. Giving vent to all the rage that had been building up inside her. He had her, used her body with his hateful, lustful filthy desires—for nothing. NOTHING! She knew with intuitive certainty that there was no play, no part. It was all a figment of his imagination. And she allowed herself to be stripped and screwed, paraded naked in front of him, bent over in front of him, screwed until she hurt —for nothing! Nothing but his vile pleasure!

Her nails ripped his face. Her hand lashed across his eyes. He was taken aback and made no move for a moment to defend himself. He put up his hand and she seized and bit it, deep, catching the immediate taste of blood. He cried out in pain and rolled away across the divan and off, falling onto the floor. Some older girl's tale came to her and she lashed out with her bare foot at the limp balls which hung to the floor under his thick, heavy penis. He jerked away just in time and her foot caught him up the behind instead, so that he cried out again and jackknifed forward, with his hand to his buttocks. He scrambled to his feet as she leapt at him again. He took two swipes across his startled face and his nose suddenly began to bleed. His fish eyes went cold, as if they had gone out. He seized her arm and threw her onto the divan. She realized how very much stronger than her he was, but her blood was up and she sprang at him as he came at her, spitting and snarling. Her nails tore red welts across his fat chest and then he'd flattened her. His weight knocked the breath out of her body. She bit the hand again which roughly swung her over onto her stomach. He slapped the back of her head with stunning force, wheezing between his teeth with the effort. He tore up the dressing gown, exposing her slim naked body with the tiny waist and beautiful round buttocks. He knelt heavily on her flawless back and began to lash her bottom with his hand with all his strength. She struggled, but she could only writhe her hips under the fury of the stinging blows which fell thick and fast across the smooth orbs of flesh, now on her buttocks, now on her thighs.

"You beast, beast, beast!" she gasped. But now he seemed like some highly efficient piece of machinery, belting her with the flat of his large hand with a force that made her rump begin to sting, to feel raw as a skinned beetroot. Her struggles weakened. She was exhausted. Tears of tired rage welled in her eyes. After a while the blows ceased and then he quickly tied her hands with the cord of the gown. She struggled again furiously. No, it couldn't be true. One person couldn't inflict such shameful indignity on another. But her hands were tied fast.

He pulled her back across the edge of the divan so that her hips rested on the edge, her legs trailing down to the floor. He pushed her thighs wide apart once again. She began to sob as he pushed his rod into her cunt yet again, half standing, half lying across her bent bottom. As his hot, fleshy staff drubbed up and up into her flayed passage, he gave a sexy, mirthless, gasping chuckle, which mingled with her sobs and then lost itself in a continuous pant of lust.

CHAPTER FIVE

"I just love these little English country towns—so very picturesque. But how anyone could want to live in them for ever and ever, I just can't begin to understand. Give me a bit of life—and people are life, interesting people, vital, creative people. They carry life with them and infuse it in the people they meet. All these others are dead, just as this quaint, charming, mediaeval town is dead. You can only look at it, beautifully embalmed, like a corpse in a New York funeral parlour and think how lovely it is and how unutterably, unshakeably and irredeemably dead. I'm sorry, Joseph. I know you live here and all that. But I remember when you had other ideas. And if you're not careful, you'll grow into a stuffed dummy just like this place."

Mrs. Gracie Goldenbaum was talking with all the confidence bred of great wealth and great reputation as a personality. The reputation was not unearned. And although the few people in the lunch-time bar in the market town could hardly be expected to agree with the opinions she was at no pains to hide or keep to her own very small group, they did at least find her, as a person, entertaining. It wasn't often you got anyone quite so obviously fearless and outspoken and colourfully sophisticated as Mrs. Goldenbaum, twice divorced, once from the great surrealist painter Simon Earpit, once from that talented writer Pieter Hansohl and many times separated from many famous liaisons in addition. She herself was a well known patroness of the arts, but not everyone trusted her judgment and nowadays she hadn't quite so much money to give quite so many parties and keep her name in the Press. She could help painters enormously, as she always had done, but she no longer had the power to make or break them.

Joseph Grant, the art master, smiled self-effacingly at her tirade. She was incapable of offending him. He'd always adored her, from the time he'd first met her at Raoul Dufy's studio many years ago—and she liked him well enough or she wouldn't have broken her journey from New York to Paris to see him.

"People like you never get older, Gracie," he said. "But people like me do and we have to take it quietly."

"Anybody who lives in a morgue will grow old with the morgue," she said. "You don't really know what's good for you, Joseph. You only think you do. You don't realise how short life is. You really have to fill the unforgiving minute unless you're going to sit in a rocking chair full of regrets for the last ten years."

She glanced at Adam.

"You listen to what I say, young man. Handsome boy like you shouldn't come under the influence of an old fuddy-duddy like Joseph. He might be a good teacher of painting, but when it comes to Life with a capital L, he's as out of his depth as a cocktail in a sewer. What did you say your name was?"

"Adam Blythe."

"Adam. That's a good name for a start. You can't go right with a name like that so you'll be all right."

Her eyes lingered on him.

"Well let's have another and then we'll take a look at these paintings of yours."

Adam drank his Scotch. He didn't normally touch it; couldn't afford it, but she'd insisted. He was quite fascinated by her. She was no oil painting, he told himself with a grin. But she was very well preserved and her exuberance and that hint of ever-present sensuality gave her rather piquant Jewish looks a quality of elan which many younger women would have envied. She was thin, too, which was a help to a Jew and, rather unusual—quite sinewy. And she was beautifully dressed in a thoughtless sort of way, without any jewellery at all. He wondered if she'd like his paintings. After all she'd not only studied, but had lived with and loved with some of the most famous artists of the century. Must make it rather difficult for her to adjust herself to new talents. Though he had heard tell that she supported a number of young artists of all nationalities and that the price of their work on the world's market had risen sharply due to her patronage. But one never knew how much credence to give to these stories. Such exaggerated tales grew up around all these celebrated people, particularly if they gained a reputation for never bothering to contradict anything that was said about them. Fancy old Grant knowing her like this. He'd had to look again at the old boy. What sort of wild oats had he sown in that long-lost youth?

They left the old pub and took a taxi at her insistence for the half mile to the evening class studio. Studio! A school classroom with a few easels and other gear in it. There wasn't much of Adam's work here, really. Most of it was at home in the empty attic room he used. Sitting in the taxi, he suddenly thought of Eve and wondered if she was having any luck with the agents. She'd be interested to hear about this old girl.

Mr. Grant let them into the school and led the way to the art room.

"So this is what you've come to, Joseph," she said, looking round at the desks and the meagre equipment.

"This is what I've risen to," he said. "Giving the joy of knowledge to others."

"Nonsense," she said, continuing the feud. "It's still a truism that you can't teach painting. Anyone interested can pick up the technique, as far as you can teach him, by himself with a concentrated effort. What's happened to that individuality of yours. That's all that counts in this line—and many others."

"Perhaps I should get the next plane to Paris," he said, grinning. Adam had never seen him so relaxed, nor yet so flippant.

"Perhaps! Perhaps!" She appealed to Adam. "Don't you ever give up, like this shining example. He should never have left. That's his story."

"Come on, now, Gracie," Joseph Grant said. "I was never really that good. Where was my individual voice? Some of us are meant to help along those more talented."

"How many individual voices have you known that found their special vocal cords from the beginning?" she asked. "Some people start with them, others find them at thirty, others at fifty, some much later. When you don't find them is when you give up."

"Don't keep on, you'll depress me."

Grace Goldenbaum glanced at him quickly, saw the smile and smiled back with warmth.

"Well, where are these paintings?" she asked.

Adam went to a cupboard and slid back the door. He took out three canvases. He turned them round and stood them up against the wall. They were surprising for a young painter only because one didn't expect to find such thoroughly talented and mature work stuck away in the evening classes of a local institute in the English provinces. Although in England, of course, that's where it usually is and where it usually wastes its fragrance on the desert air.

They were surrealist, which Mrs. Goldenbaum hadn't expected—as a matter of fact she hadn't expected very much at all. She had to put up with approaches like this all the time, but not often from an old friend like Joe Grant. They were well composed, electrifying in their choice of object juxtaposition, subtle in their colour blends and containing a mystic hint of other worlds.

Grace Goldenbaum stared at them for a minute or two without speaking. Mr. Grant smiled quietly to himself. Adam looked at them with a critical eye, quite forgetting that other people were looking, too.

"Hmmm." Gracie Goldenbaum was impressed. She stared a bit longer and then she said: "There's a bit of Simon in them. Do you like my old flame?"

"Yes," Adam admitted reluctantly. "But they're not so gloomy as his; the colours are more interesting and half the time he was only kidding around anyway."

Mrs. Goldenbaum looked slowly round at him with wide, amused eyes.

"Well dig that," she said. "The painter speaks."

She laughed delightedly and went closer for a detailed inspection.

"You're quite right, as it happens," she said. "A gloomier man never lived. That's why I left him. He used to sit for hours gazing at a Camembert. He hated Camembert for some reason—delicious cheese—and then all of sudden he'd pound it to a pulp with a wine bottle. There was a lot of hate in that man. There was something he felt in himself that he could never quite get to and that made him mean and moody. Sometimes he produced a fake work out of spite."

"Why don't you write your memoirs, Grace?" Joseph Grant asked. "You'd make a fortune." He laughed then at what he'd said. Imagine her needing a fortune.

"I am," she said. "First draft, eleventh chapter. I've already got a publisher."

Joseph Grant whistled in admiration.

"You make me feel older and more washed out with every word you say," he said.

"I'll dedicate it to you," she said. "Or did I promise that to Ernest Hemingway? I'll dedicate it to you anyway." She smiled another warm smile and bent down to look at the paintings.

"Well, these are good," she said, reluctantly, after a while. "Are there any more?"

"Not here," Adam said. "I have a whole heap at home."

She gave him a long, steady look. It was a different look from any she'd given him so far. She said: "Bring them round to my hotel tonight at seven. We'll have a drink and discuss what's to be done."

Grace Goldenbaum was one of those celebrities who is immediately impressed by the potentiality for celebrity in someone else. She could look at someone one minute and think: that's a good-looking person and forget it. Told that that person was so-and-so, the painter, or so-and-so, the Earl of Whatsit, she would look again and see them differently, in terms of people that were worth knowing, making an effort for, etcetera. That was how she'd looked at Adam after seeing his paintings. Suddenly he was no longer a handsome young provincial who could live and die in this "hamlet" as far as she was concerned. Suddenly he was a famous artist in embryo, another protégé, lover, lifelong addition to the legend of Grace Goldenbaum. Creative people, lords and ladies, how she loved them!

She and Joseph Grant, who had begged her to stay at his home but was not surprised at her unabated insistence on complete independence—"It means I can be generous to my friends from the heart, without feeling I owe it to them,"—watched Adam leave the school.

"He has real brilliance," she said. "What does he do apart from paint?"

"Clerking," he said. "He's one of the world's outsiders. Intelligent, quite well read, never attempted to get anything better."

"Good for him," she said. "But he mustn't waste *any* of his time on a whippersnapping job like that. I'll have to see what I can do."

CHAPTER SIX

Adam viewed his appointment at seven with mixed feelings. He didn't feel too much at ease in big hotels —and this was the only really big one in the town. And he wasn't quite sure what was expected of him. There had been something in her look...

Anyway, she'd been impressed with his work. There was no doubt about that.

Walking to the hotel, carrying a dozen of his paintings awkwardly, he glanced down at himself. Well, he'd made a bit of an effort. She should consider herself honoured. Suit for once: the new smart Italian blue, no turnups, 17-inch hem, short jacket, small bow-tie. His mother couldn't and never would understand it all. These enthusiasms for some things, unconcern about others, unexpected meetings and so on. This was what made life worth living: the unexpected boost waiting round the corner.

He went into the hotel. It wasn't so grand, really. Just a good county hotel with a few people in livery. He asked for Mrs. Goldenbaum. She'd taken one of the two suites. All the others were simply rooms, some with private bathrooms, others without.

Adam took the lift up three floors and stepped out into a short passage with a carpet which curled over his shoe welts. He followed the directions he'd been given at the desk and walked to door 22. There was a bright little highly polished knocker in the shape of a knight of King Arthur's Court. Of course the hotel was called King Arthur's Court.

He knocked solidly and after a pause the door opened.

"Hello," she said. "You're dead on time. I like people to be punctual. Everybody but me, that is."

He followed her into the suite. She was quite an eyeful. She was dressed in a simple black cocktail dress, with three rows of diamonds around her bronzed neck. Her stockings were so sheer that they shone like quartz and her black crocodile-skin shoes were long in the toe and dainty. She had a couple of Indian bangles around her right wrist which obviously had more sentimental than material value.

She led the way through the first room into another which looked almost exactly the same. The motif was rose—various shades—cool and warm from the middle rose of the carpet to the deep ruby of the velvet curtains and the deep red of the lampshades with their soft yellowish-pink tassels. The only other colours were pink rosewood and an odd bit of chrome. The effect was pretty good. Adam had had no idea there was quite such luxury in the town. From the outside one would have said untidy oak fireplaces and pebbled windows.

She took his canvases from him without looking at them and placed them against a rose-coloured wall.

"Time for them," she said. "What's yours? Scotch?"

"Champagne," he said, surprising himself. "If you have any."

She stared at him and smiled slowly.

"Sure there's champagne," she said. "I like a man who knows his own mind."

She produced a champagne bucket, glittering with ice, the bottle steamed over, enticing. She pulled the cork expertly and poured them both a large glassful. The champagne was cool and the bubbles ran up and down in it. Adam looked at it for some seconds before he raised the glass towards her. He didn't feel nervous at all. He felt a beginning of power. He felt good, as if he had finally found the world he belonged in.

She settled herself in a large, modern velvet armchair, far from the dim wall lights, and indicated another for him opposite her. It occurred to him that she'd already been knocking it back—Scotch, probably. Her cheeks were slightly flushed. In the rose light she looked positively alluring.

"Well, well," she said. "Tell me what you think. Tell me about yourself."

Adam was rather taken aback. What did he think? What was there to say about himself? But before he could answer, she said: "No, I can see you're not ready. You can tell me later. How often do you drink champagne? Do you really prefer it to Scotch?"

"It makes me lightheaded," he said. "I automatically associate it with Paris. Scotch just remains me of the local pubs and maybe a London theatre bar."

"You don't drink champagne much then?"

"Can't afford it."

"Don't make much money?"

"What do you think—I'm a solicitor's clerk."

"And hate it?"

"Naturally."

"Why not try something else?"

"Gives me a lot of spare time. Doesn't make any demands on my mind at all. Most other work would, I imagine."

"That's the way," she said. "Let's kill this bottle and have another."

They drank. He looked at the room; she looked at him.

"Would you like to see the paintings?" he asked after a bit.

"Later," she said. "I don't really need to. You have it all right."

He flushed with pleasure, felt himself flush and found the flush didn't go. He looked at the champagne. His glass was a third full. The bottle was empty.

But why, he suddenly thought, did she ask me round here if she'd already decided that my paintings were okay? He looked up at her and she smiled at him and held his eyes. Cleopatra looked at him, a Queen inviting, summoning. The flush enveloped him like a flame from the Inferno. He didn't have to think about why, looking at her. It was all clear and inevitable.

She brought another bucket of champagne and some cocktail biscuits. He began to feel quite lightheaded. He looked around the room again. This was riches. He had a quick flash of feeling about it, a real sense of glamour as if he belonged in this world as a rightful owner of it with its champagne, money, comfort, luxury, promise of the pleasures of the flesh, with way beyond it like something coming out of the mists fast cars and aeroplanes and blue seas and yachts and hot sun and long iced brandies by the palms near the beach. She carried this with her, he realised. He was so unlike Joseph Grant. Movement meant life for him: new places, new people, a new blind.

"Have you got a girl friend?" she asked suddenly. The yellow liquid cascaded from the bottle and splashed and bubbled in his glass.

"Nobody special," he said. He couldn't admit anchors in the world around him.

"Well in that case there'll be nobody to get jealous if we have a little dance, eh?"

She switched on a radiogram. He wondered if it really went with the hotel or whether it went with her. After a second, soft dance music, lush music, began to pervade the room. It was old fashioned in a way, but perfect of its type—Glen Miller in fact. He stood up and she came into his arms. She was surprisingly light and graceful and she glued her hips to his, swivelling them slightly as they turned so that she managed to massage his penis in a manner so subtle and expert that she must have been learning it since she was fifteen. He had an erection in no time and there was no hiding the fact, no need to. She put her hand round the back of his neck and stroked his hair. He put his cheek against her hair, thinking: This is working out like a woman's magazine story except for the sex.

"You're such a handsome boy," she said softly. "You'll have the world, your own world, at your feet once you get out of this rut."

"I'm nineteen," he said, "and feel much older."

"Nineteen," she said, smiling into his neck. "Youth, youth, youth, where is thy fling? Have you had many girls?"

"Had?"

"Been to bed with many?"

"Not many."

He realised suddenly that she was quivering. She moved her thighs against his loins.

"I can tell you want to go to bed with me," she said.

He didn't know what to say, dropped his hand down on her moving buttocks.

She slipped her hand down from his back between them, began to play with his penis.

"Let's take our clothes off," she said.

A little thrill squirmed through him. This rich, unfamiliar woman from worlds he'd only dreamed of—what was she saying?"

He glanced at the door.

"It's all right," she said. "It's locked—nobody will come in."

She unbuttoned his flies as they danced, to encourage him. She took both his hands and placed them on her rump, so that he was holding one of her buttocks in each hand. They were as finely-shaped and sinewy as he'd expected. Her body was very warm against him and she raised her face to his as she found his penis under the leg of his pants. He gasped at the cool pressure. He inclined his head and kissed her. She smelt of some faint jasmine perfume. Her lips gave in like a soft cushion and her tongue came into his mouth like a little darting eel. She crushed the length of her body against his and undulated furiously against him before pulling away.

She pulled off her dress. She wasn't wearing very much underneath, must have been prepared.

Adam, feeling rather self-conscious with his erection cleaving the air in front of this stranger, began to take off his clothes. He watched her undress to the last stitch. She had a well-kept body, sagging a little here and there but well dieted and highly tanned. It was the tan that gave it a sort of lustre, made it twice as good looking as it would otherwise have been. Her breasts were slightly thin and long; they swung a little from side to side as she came towards him. The muscles in her thighs rippled slightly and the bones of her hips just showed through, two tiny embossments at each side of the tuft of black hair below her navel.

He pulled off his socks and met her. It was very warm in the room but their flesh met like a touch of icewater. They both began to breathe fast. Adam thought: I dare not think about it, or it'll amaze me so much I'll just faint away into a dreaming sleep.

She ran her hands searchingly down over his body, pressing all the hollows, exploring, learning it all. She got his prick between her thighs as they swayed together to the music, and let it rest, jiggling lightly against the moist lips between her legs.

Adam ran his hands down her back. He could feel the articulated line of her backbone, suddenly blossoming out into those neat, sinewy buttocks. There was a lot of muscular strength in her body. He wondered how those strong thighs would grip.

"You beautiful, beautiful boy." she whispered. She kissed him again, writhing her hips against him. She dug her fingernails into his shoulders. He gripped her buttocks, pulling them towards him, rubbing his prick between the strong thighs.

"My god," she said. "I want you now! Put it in—quick!"

She dragged him with her to a divan and fell back, pulling him over on her in an expert manner that made him think, in passing, of a certain judo throw. Her fingers came down and guided his aching penis at her cunt. She was moaning into his face, her eyes closed, her hips grinding.

Adam entered her with a rush. He had the thought as he did that she was old enough to be his mother, but this simply added a perverse fascination to the whole thing.

His prick rode up in her, tightly at first, hurting along its whole, hard flesh—and then more easily. She let out a short howl, like an animal. He thrust right up into her so that their pelvic flesh bruised and bumped together.

She strained back under him, arching her loins up at his, lifting them both up off the divan for seconds at a time. She moaned incessantly and scratched all round her at the divan until the coverlet was screwed up in a ragdoll mess under them. She bit his lips, turned her face convulsively away, came back and bit his lips again, over and over.

"Put your fingers in my ass," she coughed.

He reached under her between the buttocks as he stroked rhythmically into her juicy quim. He spread them apart, felt the sweating down, found the puckered ring and thrust a finger in. She gave another gasp and screwed her behind back at his hand. He moved his finger around in her asshole. It was soft and fleshy. He felt his nail catch the flesh and she moaned and jerked and then came back again offering her rump for further exploration.

Adam's loins were coiled up like a spring. His penis felt monstrous, as if it were growing away from him in its own separate existence, increasing in size all the time like some fairytale beanstalk, a fairytale prick that would grow and grow and would spear her right through and come out of her mouth and go on searching around the room and out of the window. It expanded and contracted, throbbing painfully.

She held him tightly in the strong thighs, clamping them round his hips, slackening them, clamping them again.

She murmured obscenities in his face. Her own face began to turn a deep, furious colour, her neck strained back, her fingernails raked great weals across his back and shoulders.

"I'm coming," she rasped. The first time it was almost a matter-of-fact statement. And then she began to repeat it at lessening intervals until the words all ran together in a scream. She pulled back her thighs, presenting him with a stretched and widely open cavern of pink at the core of her body. Her legs squirmed up over his shoulders. She thrust her loins at him with bruising force. Her mouth opened, tried to close, couldn't, her eyes glazed, her nostrils flared. She gave a sudden thin unearthly whine and screwed herself onto his prick and held herself there while her loins worked up and down. And then she expelled her breath as if she were a diver suddenly coming to the surface at the end of her tether. She collapsed under him and went limp, only her body shaking and quivering like an animal in its death throes.

Adam felt a little apprehensive, even through his own mounting passion. He was afraid he'd injured her in some way. But after a few moments of simply lying still, moaning quietly, limply permitting him to go on sawing into her quim, she seemed to revive.

She looked at him with a long, purring look like a satisfied cat. She closed her eyes and uttered a cosy exclamation as he dug into her a little further.

"That was something," she murmured.

She gave another exclamation. She held his panting mouth with hers.

"Honey," she said, releasing his lips. "Like a damn virginal fool I've packed my pessary in a trunk that's on the high seas to Le Havre—and I'm not quite so old that I can afford not to have it. It's not fair on you, I know. But I'll do my best. Turn over."

Adam allowed hemself to be turned over on his back, coming out of her with a faint plop. His penis reached yearningly up to the ceiling. He didn't see what difference it made if he screwed her one way or the other, but he let her move him around.

She leaned over him, stroking the stiff rod, first with one hand and then with both. She brought her mouth down to it and enclosed the glans in a moist warm pressure. The very thought of what she was doing as much as the actual feeling gave Adam a sharp kick, like an injection. She held his prick with one hand, lying on his loins, while she began to suck his prick, steadily, rhythmically. Up and down and with a twisting motion of her tongue at the point of each stroke.

He tensed his loins. The sight of the action made it all the more exciting. She began to suck a little harder, sometimes giving him a little bite, or scraping his bone of thick flesh with her teeth. His penis was white under the scraping suck and bright purple at its tip.

She released his jack with her hand and put both hands under his ass, holding his buttocks while she rammed her mouth down on his penis. His prick disappeared right down her. He wondered that it didn't choke her, but she was clearly a specialist.

Her tongue, with that final swiping lick, was making the glans vibrate and pulse as if it were a beacon flashing out a code into the darkness. He stiffened his hips, crossing his legs, pressing his ankles together. He felt the movement growing in his balls, as if he wanted to piss but couldn't. He watched her face working over his abdomen, her lips being pulled out grotesquely, clinging to his staff, sucking it voraciously. He pushed his loins up at her face, arching the lower part of his body from hips to toes. His mouth worked in a sweet agony. His throat was dry. His penis felt like a huge, top-heavy tree trunk. It was a tree trunk that was being felled, growing heavier and heavier until it would suddenly fall down, down... He gasped. But what would she do when he came? He couldn't think about it. Because the moment was nearly here. It was growing, growing. Strangled noises forced their way up from his lungs through the tortured passage of his gullet. There wasn't far to go. He was coming, now, now. He writhed his hips, furiously. He seemed to be standing on his head. He saw as in a wild roundabout her face working, the lips sucking, his penis soaring, his body straining, the lights, the rose, the red, the pink, a whirl. NOW! NOW! He let out a long, high-pitched cry. He felt the needle-thin stream of sperm rush from his balls along the tube at a great, unstemmable rate. She went on sucking furiously as his load shot into her mouth and his hands sought convulsively for her head and pushed it hard at his prick...

Gradually his penis deflated in her mouth but she went on gently nibbling it, sucking every last ounce of his sperm. He gave a great sigh and flopped back, exhausted. She lay for some time with her head against his belly and then she slithered up his body and kissed him on the mouth.

"Come on, sonny," she said. "Let's eat. I have a very special meal ordered. Just get dressed and I'll ring down for them to bring it up."

Adam began to dress. He heard her on the internal telephone asking for the food to be brought up and for this wine and that wine to go with it.

"This," he said to himself softly, "is the life—the only life for me."

CHAPTER SEVEN

"And so she promised to write to me from Paris," Adam said. "She's coming back to London in a week or two and she says she'll fix something up. She has a lot of friends who run galleries."

"Do you think she will?" Eve asked. "Or is she just one of those people who promise these things and then forget all about them?"

Adam formed a picture of the previous evening's bacchanalia. That was an aspect of the affair he had not described to Eve. Mrs. Goldenbaum would want another but once he was within reach, he was sure. She had suggested he might like to come to Paris with her, but that would have presented him with too many problems and he'd regretfully declined.

"I think she's reliable if she really likes someone's paintings," he said.

"This is marvellous then, Adam," Eve said. It may be *the* break. Perhaps in a year's time you'll be famous."

"Not so fast," he chuckled. But the thought was in his own mind all the time.

He sipped his half pint of bitter with a mental grimace, remembering the champagne, the fine wines of the night before. Back to normal for the moment. Eve had a half of bitter, too. She seemed to Adam to be rather depressed today and she looked as if she'd had a late night. No luck with the agents, that was the trouble. It put a year on you every time you tried them.

"I can't stand this one-eyed town, anyway," he said suddenly. "Something had to happen soon."

Eve nodded sadly.

"Well I've decided I must have another try at the repertory here," she said. "They all say it's because I've got no experience."

"I thought old Rushton was difficult."

"I'll just have to persuade him. Maybe he'll watch me do a part.".

Eve said one thing, thought another. Rushton, the manager of the local repertory, was another Grampion, a lesser one. He, too, badly wanted to sleep with her. They were all the same. It was the only key to the door. So she'd sleep with him. That was her decision. It would be easy now, after Grampion. But this time she'd make absolutely certain that she got something out of it, and that wouldn't be difficult. Grampion was a married man. He would be scared as hell once he'd let himself in for it.

Poor Adam, she thought. He'd have a fit if he knew what I'd done, what I'm going to do. But it all seemed remote from Adam. It was, after all, business.

"I have the feeling that things will begin to change soon," she said. "They couldn't be much worse."

"I think they will," Adam said, thinking of himself. "There's so much worth having in the world. All you've got to do is make up your mind and then get it."

"We haven't been very clever about it up till now, I think," she said.

He glanced at her curiously, wondering if she'd read his thoughts, but she was thinking about the stage.

"Well to hell," he said. "To hell with this bloody bitter. Let's both have a Scotch for the sake of things to come."

CHAPTER EIGHT

Eve stood on the opposite side of the narrow main street of the town and studied the front of the local theatre. It was an old-fashioned stone building with ornate pillars framing the foyer on either side and the word "Playhouse" flamboyantly painted on a yellow board which filled the broad gable of the roof. The lights were on in the foyer, revealing several glass cases containing photographs of past productions by the repertory company. The box office was empty. They would soon be coming out, the show over, the audience racing to wolf a last drink before England's barbaric licensing laws decreed that drinking must stop for the night, unless one wanted to cart bottles home.

The nicely-designed advertisement placard on the front of the narrow theatre building showed that the company were playing "Blithe Spirit." They seldom attempted anything more ambitious. But this wasn't because they lacked ambition. It was simple economics. The theatre was small, rent was high, houses were about 70 per cent, which was good but hardly enough to keep body and soul together. A local television company gave a grant of a few hundred pounds, the Arts Council gave a few hundred more, the "enlightened" local council gave a hundred—which was a hundred more than most local councils gave—and a small but energetic supporters' club gave another few hundred raised from donations, whist drives and a big annual bazaar, regularly opened by some second-rate television star. So one had to be sure of at least that 70 per cent house. And the only way was to present harmless, superficially entertaining, safe plays. This dictum could, on occasion, be confounded. But it was a risk, always a risk and if the actors were to eat they couldn't afford to take risks more than two or at the most three times a year.

These thoughts went through Eve's head as she waited for the curtain and for the audience to stream out into the street. It wouldn't be much. In fact she wasn't interested in the parts she could or couldn't get in this little hole. The main thing was to get in and to get to know people.

Up the side of the theatre ran a small passage in which were two dustbins and a couple of bicycles. At the end of that passage was the stage door and beyond it the two dressing rooms: one male, one female, and the room which served as an office for the manager. There was also a small and completely inadequate toilet with a broken chain and no lid to the seat. None of it was a dream come true and Eve's thoughts went far beyond it. Many actors and actresses passed their lives in repertory, moving from one to another throughout the provinces, sometimes spending a couple of years in one place, never getting a bigger chance, celebrities only in the local small town—and not even very celebrated there, if one considered the small proportion of any given population which went to the theatre more than three times in their lives.

An attendant appeared in the foyer and clipped back the doors leading to the auditorium. There was a confused sound of people from inside and then the first couples began to emerge, developing into a crush of people, filling the foyer and, as always, hardly moving, aimlessly blocking the path of those yet to come out.

Eve waited until the crowd thinned a little and then she saw Rushton appear in the foyer, a tall man with a sneering, foxy face dressed in a grey tweed suit. He smiled, nodded, sometimes bowed. He thought himself a real personage.

Eve wandered over to the foyer and climbed up the four stone steps. Rushton saw her, smiled warily and turned back to someone who was trying to engage him in conversation. Eve wandered from panel to panel of the photographs which she already knew so well. She knew most of the company already. She was, after all, quite well known in amateur theatrical circles in the town and the standard was pretty high.

The crowd got thinner and thinner until finally Rushton was left with only Brigadier Jankers and Mrs. Jankers, towers of strength in the supporters' club. They knew what they liked. A good play: beginning, middle and end, with plenty of laughs preferably. None of this bolshie-angry stuff and none of this Tennessee Williams psychological muck. Real people weren't like that. Real people like them, like Brigadier Jankers and Mrs. Jankers and woe betide anyone who deviated from their honest, decent norm. Sub-norm, some people would have said. But those were the sort of people the Brigadier would have put under lock and key, or given a good spell in the Pioneers to make them understand what life was about—so they didn't worry him.

"You don't get them the calibre of Coward these days," he was saying. "All plays about nothing these days—filth and Communism (it was surprising he made any distinction) and people shouting about nothing. Rattigan's all right of course, but as for these other fools—I could write a better play myself."

"You should, Brigadier, you should," Rushton said smoothly. He was able to say things with complete ambiguity. Whichever side you were on it sounded as if he was on yours.

"Hah. Yes. Hah. Will one of these days. Surprise the old town," the Brigadier said. "Well, keep up the good work..."

Rushton bowed and said goodnight. He turned to Eve and looked at her without speaking.

"Sounds as if you might get a good play sometime," Eve said. She was completely familiar with Rushton because he was the sort of character she saw right through and felt a mild contempt for.

He smiled and put his tongue in the side of his mouth to make a bulge.

"What can I do for you?" he said. "Decided to give yourself to me body and soul?"

"Body only," she said. "You wouldn't know what to do with a soul if you had one."

He stared at her. He laughed nervously and came towards her. His reaction was different from Grampion's. He didn't really believe her.

"And you, in return, have to take me into the rep and give me a good part in the first play you haven't cast fort yet," she said. "Which I suppose means the week after next."

He continued to stare at her and then he gulped. She saw his Adam's apple move up and down.

"Come back to the office," he said. "You'd better not be fooling."

"I'm not fooling," she said.

She saw the desire in his eyes. His chest was heaving rapidly under his suit jacket. His mind started turning the situation to the auditorium and peered through to where an attendant was walking along the rows of seats looking for lost property.

"Perhaps we'd better not go to the office," he said. "I'll get my car."

"No," she said. "We'll go to the office first. I want something in writing."

"In writing?"

"Yes, I don't trust people very much."

She saw his mind groping over what this meant.

"But how can I trust you?" he asked.

She came up close to him. She pressed her hips against him. "You just can," she said.

He broke away from her, flushing.

"Careful," he said. "Careful, for god's sake."

She smiled to herself. Once he'd fucked her he'd be completely in her power. Strange that he didn't realise that. Or perhaps he did, but his desire was just too much for him.

"Come on then," he said.

He led the way through the auditorium, up the steps onto the stage, off at the wings and round the back to the office. There was a subdued chatting from the dressing rooms. He took her into the office, but didn't lock the door, after a moment's deliberation.

"All right," he said. He sat down behind the shabby desk, pretending to be businesslike for the sake of possible interruptions. He motioned her to a chair opposite.

"So what do you want," he said. "I'll have to take you on as assistant stage manager—you know, making the tea—or it'll look suspicious. But the week after next I can give you a part. We're doing *Flowering Cherry*. You can have the part of the daughter. It's not a bad one for a start. How about it?"

She reflected. Now, she really felt quite excited. The part wasn't a large one, but it wasn't a small one either. And the play was good. Robert Bolt was now respectable enough for them to put on his plays without too much risk.

"All right," she said. "Suits me."

He pulled out a form contract and added a proviso about "Flowering Cherry." He let her read it and then he signed it and she signed it. His eyes ranged all over her while she signed. He'd admired her looks for years. But he'd never really imagined...

"So where do you want payment?" she asked, matter-of-factly. She felt as if she were simply exchanging one commodity for another. He licked his lips. She could see his brain grappling with the possibilities. He'd probably have suggested a weekend if he hadn't been afraid of her changing her mind. He wanted her now, but he couldn't think where.

"We'll go for a drive," he said. "It's too dangerous here."

"All right," she said.

He got up and she stood up. He came round the desk and caught hold of her. He kissed her and she responded coolly. He rubbed his palms over her breasts under her coat. He was sweating at the temples. He turned away from her abruptly and brushed back his hair nervously.

What a seducer, she thought. If his wife so much as telephoned now, he'd have a blue fit.

"All right," he said aimlessly. "Right."

He opened the door gently.

"Let them all go and I'll lock up," he said. "I'll pick you up on the corner by the Crown."

She grinned at the way she was becoming a street corner clandestine. She felt cool and clear headed. At least she was really getting *something* out of this. It gave her a sense of achievement.

She left the theatre and stood for a few minutes on the street corner, looking back at the theatre. She saw a group of the cast leave and set off in the opposite direction. And then the front of house girls came out and walked towards her. She turned into the doorway of a shop and studied the objects in the window: beds, appropriately enough. The girls passed, chattering, and she stepped out from the doorway and watched them go. Everything would be shortly closing up in the town. Last drinks were being called. Then there would only be the two expresso bars, the transport cafe and the two decent restaurants that stayed open until 11.30. There would be the bus queues and the emptying cinemas and the lonely policemen on their beats, a few passengers from the late night train from Waterloo.

Rushton's black Ford Consul came gently down the street. He pulled over to the corner beyond her. That was so that he could see down the other street, in case anyone was coming.

She crossed the road and he snapped open the door. She got in and he leapt away from the kerb and headed through the side streets of the town towards the open country.

"Where are we going?" she asked.

"We'll just have to find a quiet spot," he said. "I can't take you home. There's nowhere else to go."

She sat back in the car, letting the darkness race by outside like a wild dream. This, she felt, was the first real step. How ridiculous of her not to have taken it before.

"What made you decide to... to," Rushton couldn't think how to put it and ended lamely.

"To let you screw me?" She suddenly felt much more experienced, much stronger, than him.

He broke the brief silence with a laugh.

"The soul of delicacy," he said.

"Let's call a spade a spade," she said.

They drove fast and far. He kept slowing at every likely-looking layby, but he was clearly scared. Police cars passed occasionally, people out for a drive. Someone might recognise him. Scandal!

After a while she said: "Are we going to the Continent?"

He titered and then said: "Why, do you want it that badly?"

She was about to make a suitable retort when it occurred to her that she might badly overplay her hardboiled exterior. And in fact, she didn't feel quite so hardboiled now. Shortly he would find somewhere to pull in and then she'd be forced to go through all those intimate things with him. It was embarrassing if she allowed her imagination to dwell on it; it made her stomach flutter.

He turned up a little lane eventually, with the comment: "We'll see where this goes."

It didn't go anywhere to judge by fifteen minutes driving, just meandered through wood and meadow and eventually he pulled in by a five-barred gate, leaving just room for the unexpected vehicle to pass. The engine went dead and he turned off the headlights, leaving them in darkness with the moon-silvered field around them. He turned towards her and she turned her face at his. His breath had a hot, winy smell as his mouth closed on hers. He held her face in his hands and ran his lips all over it and then his tongue.

"You lovely creature," he kept repeating.

And then his hands started moving all over her inside the coat, weighing her breasts, gripping her buttocks, pinching her waist and smoothing her back. He undid the buttons of her blouse, breathing asthmatically through his nose. He felt her breasts with trembling hands. She melted in a little shiver. He tried clumsily to undo the brassiere, lost patience and pulled the cups off the breasts, which poked suddenly and cheekily out below. His legs moved around on the car seat. One hand went away and she sensed rather than saw it fumbling with his trouser buttons.

"Hold that," he said tensely after a second.

He took her hand and moved it over onto his lap. Her fingers encountered the upstanding sticky flesh, sticky with lubricant from his passion. She held it limply for a moment and then she began to stroke and caress it mechanically. She felt now almost in a state of shock. Her sangfroid had deserted her. Was it really happening all over again?

His hands came back onto the flushed bulbs of her breasts. He stroked them at first tenderly, so that the pores of the skin seemed to open to his fingers, and then more roughly as he began to push his loins in time with her caressing hand. He kissed her again, hard and wetly and then he buried his face in her clothes and she felt his lips sucking at her breasts, pulling at the skin all over the pears, as if, indeed, they were ripe fruit. He hurt her a couple of times but she gritted her teeth and bore the pain. It was beginning to unsettle her. She found herself moving her buttocks on the seat; she felt heat between her legs and under her armpits.

Then she felt his hand on her leg. He stroked the stockinged calf, digging his fingers into it, then holding it lightly as if he wanted fully to get the feel of it. And then his hand started to move away, up the warm stockinged leg to her knee. He fondled the underside of her knee for a moment and then went on, advancing slowly, without opposition, up the thigh until he reached the point where the silk covering ceded to soft, filmy flesh. He caught his breath and moved on. His prick was jumping in her hand, jerking with a life of its own and his loins were heaving like a chest after great physical effort.

He came to the frill of her briefs, murmured her name, jiggled towards her and went on into the wet crevice. She gave a little gasp and flattened her crutch against the seat, holding his hand trapped, unable to move. He jiffled his fingers around in the wet little pit until she relaxed. He pushed his fingers further up her quim and now she leaned her torso backwards and thrust her loins forward towards him, releasing his prick.

Breathing in a sort of broken morse code, he pulled at her girdle, somehow getting it undone; he pulled the briefs off her legs and she kicked her shoes into the front of the car.

"Let me take my skirt off," she said. "I'll get creased."

She slipped out of the garment while he wriggled out of his trousers and pants. And then he came back at her, groping for her loins, running his hands all over them as if he wanted to savour every millimetre. She felt quite hot and lustful now and she reached under his shirt and stroked his testicles and pinched his prick with tiny nibbling pressures.

"Let's get out," he suggested hoarsely. "There's not room in here."

Without waiting for her answer he knelt up and reached over the seat for his coat in the back. She drew her sharp fingernails down the underside of his stiff penis and then opened the car door. She stepped out onto the cool tarmac, wearing only her blouse and her stockings with the girdle hanging down. She stood uncertainly in the lane looking along it into the darkness and then he followed her in his shirt and socks with his penis reaching out like a boom and protruding from under the hem.

"The field," he said.

The field was cut off by the gate and a six-foot hedge. It meant climbing over the gate. She felt her embarrassment now. It meant presenting him with her bare rump as she got over. He put a hand on her buttocks.

"Come on," he said, "quickly."

She put a foot on the bottom bar and climbed up. He gave her behind a lustful slap and then shoved his index finger inside her as she swung one leg over. She jumped down to the grass on the other side. It was damp to her stockinged feet. I'll get pneumonia, she thought.

Rushton followed her and she watched his balls swing like a kilt as he levered himself over the top, his penis sticking out above them like a long, searching, dangerous cannon.

He led the way along the back of the hedge, just a few yards, and then he arranged his coat, grabbed her by the waist and practically forced her down onto it. He was in a hurry to get inside her now and he dropped down on her as she lay down, surging into her with a gasp almost before her back had touched the ground. His thrust almost took her breath away. She felt wet, hot and vulnerable with that space between her legs. She really felt she wanted it inside her. If he'd left her now she would have gone mad.

But such thought of leaving was far from his mind. He was scrabbling and shoving to get farther and farther inside her, as if to ram up into her and pierce her womb were his only desire.

His hips danced against her upturned buttocks. She pulled her thighs high under him and bit her lip. This was different from before. Was this familiarity breeding know-how and desire? His thighs were hot on the undersides of hers. She could smell the wetness of the grass around them and see the moon, sleek and bright in the sky. The strange, airy openness of it all added to her sense of being completely free, a child of nature to do exactly as she pleased.

Their grunts and moans mingled together like smoke and steam and their bodies writhed like one with two heads, four arms and four legs. Once she thought: If anybody passed now and stopped, we just wouldn't hear them. And would it matter?

She felt his flexing thrust become suddenly furious, as if he were going to shoot a load of semen into her and then he suddenly relaxed, pulling himself up with an effort. He came out of her and she felt acute disappointment. So much so that she caught hold of his penis and tried to pull it back into her.

"What's up, for god's sake?" she whispered.

"I haven't got any contraceptives on me," he gasped. "I nearly came."

She hadn't even been able to think of it. She grimaced to herself. But now that he was out of her she cooled a little. She was really very stupid taking these risks, she realised. But she was astonished that he was concerned. And then she realised. He could hardly deny paternity—

at least not without going through the courts. Imagine the scandal, the inconvenience.

She reached down and massaged his prick. It was wet with her own juices.

"Why haven't you got any contraceptives?" she said in mock annoyance.

"It's not every day I get this sort of offer," he said.

"Well," she said, "what are we going to do?"

He rubbed up against her. He bit her nipples and rolled his loins on her until she hissed with fresh desire.

"Turn over," he whispered. "I'll make love to you in your bottom."

She was sufficiently roused with passion not to consider his proposal as complete lunacy or to be wholly disgusted. She had heard that people did this sort of thing. It avoided kids. She remembered it had even come out in connection with the homosexual part of the Wolfenden Report that 15 per cent of married couples in Britain made love sometimes that way to avoid pregnancy. It was supposed to be quite exciting for the woman; something to do with a gland there was inside. But surely very painful.

"I don't know," she said. "I don't know..." She couldn't think what to say. And it was getting colder and she was aware of the dampness of the field around them.

He stroked the inside of her thigh right up to the wet opening of her cunt.

"You agreed to let me make love to you," he said. "You're lucky I just didn't go straight on and get you knocked up."

"That wouldn't have suited you either," she said, and then gave a sharp grunt as his fingers found her clitoris. He lowered his head to her body and ran it down her belly. He nibbled the soft protuberance of flesh just under the navel, gathering it into his mouth in a thin roll. He moved on down and licked her thighs. And then he found the fleshy tunnel and thrust his tongue into it. She gave a gasp and then another as his lips closed on the hard little clitoris. She strained her hips up at his mouth, arching her back and gritting her teeth. She had an enormous desire to come into his mouth. She revolved her hips in a grinding, circular motion with a push at his lips every time the motion reached the six o'clock position.

"Don't stop," she pleaded. "Don't stop!"

And at that he bit her clitoris, making her scream. She felt as if the walls of her womb were peeling off. All of a sudden all her inside was crumbling away like a house falling in.

"Go on!" she panted. "Go on!"

And then there was a rushing in her ears and she choked and the house fell right in with a great resounding and echoing crash and she screamed at the sweet, intolerable delight of it and wanted it to go on for ever and never stop.

When it was over and she lay gasping and slowly recovering, he turned her over. She didn't resist. Her will power seemed to have been drained out of her with the orgasm. He kissed her smooth, oval buttocks and bits them with sharp little nips. He drew them apart with his hands and licked the crevice between them. She felt the stain on her asshole as he pulled the skin around it. She felt obsceneiy naked with him hovering above the deep red little hole, but it didn't matter any longer. Nothing seemed to matter; there was no embarrassment.

She felt his finger probing the little puckered inlet.

"Spread your legs," he ordered.

She spread her legs out, so far that the toes of her stockinged feet touched the grass on either side of the coat. His finger prodded. She winced and strained at it and suddenly it had entered. It didn't hurt very much at all; it was rather pleasant.

He moved it around in her rectum, expanding the anus. He began to saw it in and out in preparation for what was to follow. She wriggled her hips. She felt she wanted to fart, but couldn't.

After a time he dug another finger into the hole and this time it hurt her, enormously, and she bounced away. But he came after her, pinning her down with one hand in the small of her back. She felt like a mounted insect. The finger stayed in her anus, still for a time and then it began to intrude and move with the other one. She wriggled more. Once she'd got used to the extra pressure, it wasn't too bad. In fact she felt subjugated in a way that appealed to her deeply in some unexpected and, to her, rather mysterious manner.

She could feel him deliberately stretching her asshole. It hurt quite a bit every time he made a sharp, sudden movement of his fingers, but now she wanted him to get in her and do the thing properly.

"Do it," she called, turning her head to one side so that he looked down on her flushed face with the hair strewn over it. "Screw me there."

He pulled his fingers out of her. They seemed to come out reluctantly, the rubbery skin of the anus clinging to them until they came out with a sucking noise.

She felt his hot body come down on hers and stretch out along its length. She shivered with anticipation. Then he changed his mind and kneeled up between her thighs.

"Kneel up," he said.

Obediently she kneeled up, presenting him with the stretched moons of her buttocks, bending away before him as she had in front of Grampion.

She felt his hands close on the tops of her thighs, gripping them tighly. And then one hand went away and pushed her arms between her legs so that she could reach his balls. She held them and stroked them for a second and then he said: "Place it for me."

She took hold of his penis. It felt enormous. It was really much bigger than two fingers. She strained outwards and placed the blunt cudgel at the opening of her backside. She felt it prodding and working against her anus. It was going to be much too big. She suddenly felt that with certainty. Now the tip of it had found the comparatively tight aperture and was worming its way into it. It was all right, all right... and then suddenly she felt as if a tree trunk were trying to burst into her body.

She pulled away, but he held her tight and persisted.

"Oh no, no!" It hurts!" she cried.

But he ignored her pleas. He held her now in a bear hug and just pushed and pushed.

"It's too big! It won't ever go in!" she screamed.

She couldn't escape from him. His thighs thrust her thighs forward; his arms held her hips back at his. She was helpless.

"Push back!" he yelled.

She could hardly think. Every way was pain and more pain. She pushed back and opened her ass, as if by deliberate effort, that final centimetre. It was like flicking a plaster off a wound: the quicker the better. His penis surged right into her rectum, solid and very painful, but now better because there was no more to go.

"Oh, oh, oh!" she gasped.

It was like having her asshole shored up with huge

supports, like a mine that would collapse if they were moved.

Now gasping and crooning with delight he began to saw rhythmically and without the slightest mercy deep up into the soft confines of her back passage.

Gradually the pain eased a little, though it was still a mixture of hurful discomfort and stimulation. She felt strangely wet between her buttocks and also strangely ashamed. She had never expected to be sodomised and there seemed something not quite decent about it, something rather debasing. But every time these thoughts crept into her head, they were hurled right out again by a skin-splitting thrust which jolted her forward and made her squirm back onto the rod which was meting out the punishment. She began to feel a masochistic joy. The pain was weirdly pleasurable. She began to move backwards to meet the forward thrust of his loins. She began to undulate her body and move her buttocks in tiny circles. She even began to feel quite excited through the pain and she reached under her and scratched his swinging balls gently, turning her face sideways just so that he could see the effect he was having on her.

Kneeling above her, Rushton watched the reddish skin of the little round hole draw back with his prick, clutching it as if it didn't want him to come out. At first the pressure on his cock had been almost too much to bear, but now it was just tight and exhilarating. The sort of squeeze that promised to pull the sperm right out of his tube like a dozen razor blades at every thrust.

He watched his white, furious penis disappear right up her ass with every stroke. It went right in so that not a half inch of it showed and then it moved about in that tight, resistant passage with the knob straining out as if it were going to burst like a boil.

There was a speck of shit on the rough edge of her anus where his rod entered it and the skin against his prick already looked inflamed.

His balls ached and his penis danced with a thousand hot sparks every time he surged into her, and she herself was moaning and adding to his pleasure by the movement of her bottom and the hollowing of her back. He watched her face as his lips drew back from his teeth. Her beautiful face was flushed crimson in the moonlight, dark in the moonlight, and her shoulders shook in time with the fishlike opening and closing of her full mouth. Her long, blonde hair fell over her face and flopped around her neck as she squirmed. She was completely his. A slave, submitting to him. He could do with her anything he liked and he did, digging his penis into her ass and leaving it there, hearing her groan while he simply joggled his loins and moved it gently around in her channel like a probing, hard-bodied snake.

"Oh, yes," she breathed. "Go on!"

He drew it out to the glans and then plunged it right in again in one long, slow stroke. His prick was tingling, his balls alive. He could come now whenever he chose and he wanted to feel that rush of sperm into her ass; that would be the ultimate submission.

He began to rub rapidly into her, hard and fast, battering her quivering buttocks with his hips. He gripped her waist hard with his fingers, squeezing the spare flesh into odd shapes. His mouth opened and wouldn't close again. His breath whirled out of it in long, broken gasps, like that of a man rowing. He stared at her slender body as he spread the thighs wide and pulled her buttocks apart even more with his hands. He wanted to skewer her like a carcase, split her body wide open. His prick was huge and heavy, loaded with weight as if it had ripened in the last seconds.

"My god!" he groaned. "My god!"

His shirt got in his way and he tore at it convulsively with sharp, jerky movements, like a puppet. His fingers scratched her buttocks hard, grabbing the flesh in handfuls. He touched her anus with his fingers, feeling the heat of friction where his cock drubbed in. She was murmuring incoherently and turning her face from side to side on the blanket of his coat. He pulled her back onto his staff like fitting a boot. His prick was swollen and bloated like a body three days in water. It was like a balloon, a balloon full of intensity. He gasped, choked out her name, gasped again, gave a last spine-chilling ramrod thrust and shattered his sperm in wave after wave into the depths of her behind. It seemed as if his scrotum had never been emptied before. He groaned and almost cried with excruciating delight...

Some minutes later he got up from his kneeling position against her backside. He wiped his penis on the grass. The field and the moon and the nearby lane and the car all swam back into the picture. He glanced at his watch. God, they'd been a long time!

"Better go," he said.

The girl straightened up as if she'd been asleep.

"That hurt," she said accusingly.

They stood up and went to the car. They both felt ridiculous standing nearly naked in the lane. They dressed quickly and he turned the car with some difficulty and they headed back to the town.

"You can start when you like," he said, after a while.

"I'll have to give a week's notice," she said.

They drove on in silence. Her bottom ached now. Her back passage was sore as hell.

"I'll make sure I get my money's worth for this," she told herself. And she gave a little wintery smile in the darkness.

CHAPTER NINE

"But it's so dangerous," Rushton said. "Don't you understand how dangerous it is?"

"It may seem dangerous to you, but to me it's just something I'm not going to miss—not for anything."

"What do you mean—not going to miss. It depends on me if I take you."

"If you don't take me, you know what I told you I'd do."

"I don't believe it. You wouldn't be such a bitch. And in any case it would affect you too."

Eve smiled at Rushton. She didn't have to press her point. He knew she had the whip hand.

It was midweek, lunchtime. He had driven her 30 miles to a distant town so that they wouldn't be seen having lunch together. Later he would drive her back and drop her on the bus route and then they'd meet later at the theatre where she was having a big local success in *Flowering Cherry*. Their attitude in company together was of friendly banter and comparative indifference. They played their parts well. So well, in fact, that nobody seemed to have guessed that her sudden entry into the ranks of the repertory was more than persistent soliciting on her part and an eventual recognition of her quite apparent talent. The public took to her looks; the company found her a good but inexperienced actress. She was unlikely, they felt, to reach higher levels.

Rushton was infatuated with her, she could tell. But he was annoyed with himself for being so. Half the time he was pleading, half the time bullying. Very, very occasionally she let him drive her out into the field and enjoy a repeat performance of the tender delights her charms could give him. Very occasionally. In fact, every time he gave evidence of being so exasperated that she feared he might try to kick her out rather than put up with the torment. She enjoyed sex with him occasionally, but most of the time she was aloof. She used him as she needed him. And now she needed him to take her to the London party he'd been boasting about for some days. It was a party being given by a repertory company on the ringe of Central London. They were one of the best reps in the country; members were always being taken into West End productions. They got a bigger grant from the Arts Council than most and they even had a special dispensation from the Gulbenkian Foundation—the only repertory in the country for this distinction. Of course, they were no better off materially than most repertory companies—worse than many. They produced in a converted church hall which held an audience of about 150 people on hard canvas chairs, the canvas stretched over tubular frames. There was no bar, and coffee in the interval behind the petition at the back of the auditorium just seemed to emphasise how very cold it always was in the theatre. But they were very good, and they had this reputation.

The party was being given in honour of their twentieth anniversary and they'd invited a few friends from the provinces. Rushton had been manager there before moving to the greater material comfort of his present post. No actors of any great note were going to be at the party, but at least one famous drama critic and a couple of the new young playwrights had promised to turn up. This had been enough for Eve to determine that she was going to be there. The environment of London was enough to raise her blood pressure; to be in theatrical circles there, even if they weren't the highest, was like a shot of cocaine.

But Rushton had been difficult. Some of them knew him up there. They didn't know his wife but they might think it strange. She might bump into one of them some day. Who could tell?

She had cut right through his arguments. She was going and that was all and if he didn't agree, then his wife would begin to hear things she shouldn't. He'd fought a desperate losing battle, as much against himself as against her, as in many ways he wanted her to come—and there was a chance they might be able to spend the night together. This thought gave him goose flesh. He wanted to see just how many times he was still capable of performing the act in the same night; he wanted to have her naked against him in the cosy, long-lasting warmth of a bed, away in a strange hotel where nobody knew them and there could be no fear at all of discovery, no anxieties. But he was a little frightened of her determination. Her self-possession often disturbed him. He would have liked her to be madly in love with him, prostrate at his feet. He'd had one or two affairs since his marriage, but they'd been with older women, married women. And they'd either been more lukewarm than this or he'd been in command of the situation. This time, although he never dared admit it to himself in so many words, she had all the power in the world to hurt him. And although he hid this from her frantically, it often seemed that she knew it and, worse, that she didn't give a damn. He was seldom allowed to intrude in her private life. He knew she had a boy friend, but she wouldn't even say if the boy friend had an inkling about him. He was both jealous and helpless. The only time he could pretend he dominated was when he had her moaning under him. Then he gritted his teeth and really gave it her, imagining he was hurting her, paying her back for her rebellion. But alas, the moment passed, and he saw that she'd enjoyed her own sexual fulfilment in a little whirl of passion which had nothing to do with him personally. It was as if he were the slave serving his powerful mistress and then being banished to the stables.

He tinkled his spoon nervously in his empty coffee cup. He looked up at her, thanking heaven that he had these moments when, at least, she was with him alone and forced to direct her attention on him, even if it was only to dismay and menace him.

"All right," he said, slowly. "I'll have to say I met you in town and brought you along. It'll look bloody suspicious, but nobody'll be able to prove otherwise. And then we need never mention it unless something totally unexpected happens to throw it in our faces."

"That's right. It's simple, really."

She smiled across the table at him and put her hand on his. The gesture made him feel better. He looked forward to the Saturday, to the long time alone with her, to the possible night. The party itself became meaningless.

CHAPTER TEN

Somewhere in the background Lottie Lenya was singing snatches from the *Threepenny Opera* in German, but the wonderful voice was almost drowned in the hum of conversation, the movement from bottle to bottle, the clink of glasses, the coming and going throughout the house. They had arrived when the party was well under way. They'd had several drinks on a tour of London bars to brace her for the ordeal of meeting the sort of people she'd never really met before outside the small circle of the home town rep. She felt slightly high and gazed around the house in delight. It belonged to the chairman of the directors of the company which owned the theatre—a Sir Hugh Cassidy-Cox, who had once written his own play which the company had dutifully performed, and who liked to think of himself, old bachelor as he was, belonging to the young, creative set, being a regular bohemian. Nobody could say he lacked generosity.

He was fixing drinks for several people now—for those who preferred not to help themselves. A round, chubby man with grizzled grey hair and crinkled, sharp eyes, he listened to everyone's conversation at once, chuckling and agreeing and making suggestions and then suddenly coming out with something so reactionary that nobody could even take him seriously. Except that he was serious, for he'd never allowed his interest in the theatre to rid him of any of his prejudices, which were all of the most solid Victorian variety. But he had to be tolerated or the theatre might fall around the ears of the actors. So they drank and were merry and turned away from him when they wanted serious conversation.

Eve accepted a drink from someone and looked around the room into which they'd come. They'd entered through a little courtyard from the street and come straight through French windows into a delightful room with modern furniture and paintings and a stairway running up one side of it to the floor above. There was a huge log fire in a very large grate and the cigarette smoke was thick. Someone wandered in from a room on the right carrying two more bottles of Scotch and dragging a crate of beer. Low voices came down from the stairs where all was in darkness.

Rushton was cut off from her and she was left contemplating a couple of paintings for a moment. Nobody was ready to jump up from established conversation and comfort to make a beeline for the attractive girl who'd just arrived. That would have been a little too corny.

She caught snatches of conversation:

"I thought your answer to Noel Coward was very good; really that man is a supreme idiot." ... "So is your new play going to be more or less a sequel to 'The Voice of the Herd'?" ... "I just dislike playing those roles where everything's laid on for you. Look at O'Toole as Private Bamforth—very good, of course, but he couldn't do more than act out a rigid type, the barrack room lawyer. Give me a more subtle part every time." ... "Oh, there's money in television all right and there's no need to move over full time." ... "Yes, Sir Michael invited me to the first night. He told me to go backstage afterwards; some sort of party..."

She felt a thrill of longing and apprehension. She glanced surreptitiously at the speakers. She began to place them. That would be Edwin Fryer, who was making such a name for himself with his Royal Court plays. And that would be James Harrod, the famous drama critic. How young he was, and handsome! And he'd already travelled over half the world for his newspaper and been invited as guest critic to half a dozen publications in other parts of the world. And that face she'd seen in character parts in films. And they all looked so vital, as if they were all going somewhere, not just stagnating and slowly dying in a little provincial slough.

"I'd like you to meet Eve Patten..."

She turned from the paintings. Rushton was approaching with a big, bearded man in a check shirt with a hairy chest visible at the open front. Here we go, she thought. This is the beginning of Eve Patten's bid for stardom.

Two hours and many gins later she found herself sitting in a corner with the famous drama critic. At first she hadn't heard a word he'd said just out of dazzlement at the proximity of a celebrity, but now she was listening and doing her best to keep up with him, feeling very young and inexperienced, but trying hard not to show it. It didn't seem to worry him, anyway. He was content to talk to a willing and, indeed, fascinated listener.

More people had come and there was dancing going on in what seemed like the far reaches of the room. Actually it was a few feet away, but drink had lent distance to everything. Sometimes she glanced up to see who was looking and noticed the figures swaying thickly together, licentiously many of them—there was a lot of undisguised mauling going on—or squatting on the floor, on divans, clustered in groups around chairs, dozing, chattering, drinking, nibbling food. Rushton was deep in conversation with the bearded man, having made full circle and come back to him. But not so deep that he failed to cast a possessive eye in Eve's direction every five minutes.

It hadn't taken Eve long to realise that, in spite of the greater fame of the two playwrights present, the drama critic was the man with far and away the most influence. He knew the most people; his opinion was law for a great many.

"Of course," James Harrod was saying, "all these plays suffer badly in translation. You find that even in such obvious things as the titles. I mean 'Huis Clos'—'Vicious Circle' ... 'In Camera', no, neither; the words are untranslatable as an identical concept and you find exactly this point on the more serious level of values and attitude. It's difficult for so many of us to accept that purity of Anouilh's. It crosses the Channel badly. It has nothing to do with morality, but with keeping one's own nature strong and clear, preserving it in a pure state..."

His voice went on, a beautiful voice which roamed among the words so easily and fluently. She had the feeling that she could ask him about absolutely anything and he'd be able to give her a long and detailed answer without any hesitation at all. She toyed with funny questions in her mind—"Tell me about West Highland Terriers"—so that she nearly giggled at her own thoughts. Being a good drama critic must involve so much more knowledge and powers of analysis than ever a playwright needed, she realised.

She looked up at him and his eyes devoured hers as he talked. His voice went on ranging over his thesis, but she could tell that he was looking at her too as a woman. She let her skirt move up her thigh a little and his eyes flicked away to the leg and back again to her face without there being a break in his words.

They drank their liquor and he went on talking while she listened.

"...you ought to meet some of these people," he said. "I'm sure you'd find them interesting—and you can never know too many people when you're trying to create opportunities for yourself."

Her ears went back. This was the sort of language she understood immediately.

"I should like that very much," she said. Her hand brushed his arm as she put down her glass, apparently accidentally. She looked into his eyes and repeated: "Yes, I really would like that."

He seemed about to say something more when Rushton came over. Rushton beamed at him and got a lukewarm response, but, not put off, he joined in the conversation with them for a few minutes before he was pulled away by somebody else. The critic began to discourse about another topic. The chance had been lost.

After a time he put down his glass.

"Call of the wild," he said. "Don't go away."

He stood up, stretched and climbed up the stairs to the storey above. She let Rushton see her sitting alone, smiled at him, waited for him to return to his conversation and then stood up. She edged round the fringe of the body of dancers, noting on the way that one girl had both hands down inside the waist of her husband's trousers, and began to climb the stairs.

Several rooms led off a landing at the top. She heard the obvious gasps of lovemaking coming from a couple. Another had the door open and beyond its darkness she saw a thin streak of light coming from under a door. That must be the bathroom. She peered into the dark room. There was a bed in the corner and a couple were smooching on it. They paid no attention to her.

She waited in the light of the landing until she heard the cistern being flushed in the bathroom. The door opened throwing a flood of light across the intervening room and the critic came out. She moved forward and he saw her.

"The call of the wild is strong tonight," she said, moving towards him.

The ambiguous words were an invitation and he accepted without hesitation. He turned the light out in the bathroom and pulled her into the shadow. He kissed her, enveloping half her face in his mouth and straining her body to his until she was almost breathless.

"Let's make love," he whispered, as he ran his lips over her willing face. His hands felt her body all over. He grabbed her by the buttocks and pulled her hips at his as he bent her backwards.

He drew her towards the bed and then he saw the couple already in occupation.

"Fuck!" he said.

She resisted then, very gently.

"I'm with someone," she said.

He didn't seem to hear.

"Let's go back to my place, baby," he said, reaching out to hold her breasts.

"I'm with someone," she insisted. "I can't possibly."

She kissed him, putting her tongue in his mouth and rubbing her hips against his.

"Why don't you take me to one of the parties where I can meet some people," she said. "We can have a ball afterwards."

She sensed him hesitate. He wasn't short of attractive women. But, of course, she was new. If he'd had her now that would have been the end of it. She understood that only too well, sure as she was that he hadn't even the vaguest idea of her name.

She put her hand on his buttocks and that seemed to decide it for him.

"All right," he said. "Give me a ring."

He thought better of that.

"No let's make it a date. There's a party next week with Sir George and Lady Celia Duncan. Call me Tuesday lunch time and we'll fix it."

He gave her a card with his name, address and telephone number. He didn't ask where she came from. She supposed he thought she lived in London.

"My name is Eve," she said. "Eve Patten. I haven't got a card—you'll have to remember."

"Eve Patten," he repeated.

She sensed him smile in the darkness.

"That's a good name," he said. "Well Eve, bring your apples with you next time. A basket load."

She let the back of her hand rest against his prick, as if by accident. She could feel its hardness. He pressed against her, gave her a fierce French kiss and then walked away to the landing.

Eve went into the bathroom and looked at herself in the mirror. She made up her lips and meditated, trying to keep as calm as possible. As long as he didn't forget or change his mind, things were working out wonderfully. She looked at her body in the full-length mirror. It was serving her very well at the moment. She left the bathroom and went downstairs. James Harrod was talking to another group of people across the room and she made no effort to approach him.

She joined Rushton, who looked at her, smiling, pleased that she came to him as if it was the natural thing to do. Perhaps, he thought, she was finally succumbing to him. He'd put the finishing touches to her tender submission in the hotel bed tonight, that he would. He grinned, with the Scotch inside him. All was right with the world.

CHAPTER ELEVEN

Adam read and re-read the letter. It was written on blue notepaper that had the appearance of cloth. It ended with kisses. He studied the envelope with the attractive French stamp—a view of a beauty spot instead of the unimaginative, interminable head of the English stamps. The stamp conjured up the city: Paris with all the glamour attaching to the name. He saw a dream city and he saw Mrs. Goldenbaum—a dream woman—from it. And now, good as her word, she was plucking him from the ugly pettiness of this little town and pulling him up there with her in the world of dreams. The invitation was for next week. He was to come to the Dorchester where she would be staying and he could stay in her suite with her for the weekend. They were to meet Leon Dalmain, one of the most influential gallery owners, at a party on the Saturday night. There would be an art critic or two and even a painter or two as well. All this she mentioned in brief. The letter was mostly about what they would do in her suite at the Dorchester, in the bedroom, in the bed. She told him what a wonderful fuck he'd given her, how she was looking forward to licking his prick again, how she wanted him to do this and that to her.

He smiled to himself. A pleasure, he thought. At your service, Ma'am, as long and as often as you like, always provided you help me up that ladder.

Adam put the letter down on the table beside his bed. He'd received it a couple of days ago and the big problem seemed to be how to explain his being away to Eve. He'd finally decided simply to pass Mrs. Goldenbaum off as a man. To his surprise, Eve had made no difficulty at all. She had almost seemed relieved that he wasn't going to see her at the weekend, said something about an awful lot of work she had to do for the next repertory production. They hadn't been seeing quite as much of each other lately. Of course, now that she had this particular job with no set hours, she was often caught up in rehearsal, or in simply learning her part, or in some activity of the theatre. They'd been out a couple of times in the last week or so. She seemed a little tired, a fact he put down to the great amount of work she was doing. He'd tried hard, after the night at her aunt's, to get her to let him screw her, but she just wouldn't quite give in, although she did toss him off now, not seeming to mind that his semen went all over her stockings or her skirt as they lay together in some field. He couldn't really understand why she wouldn't let him have her. It seemed like some strange sort of virginal pride which contrasted strangely with her broad-minded attitude to most things. She pretended to be afraid of the consequences, but she wouldn't let him do it even right after her period, using a contraceptive. His desire for her increased the more she refused him. He'd seen her naked, he'd caressed her body, her quim, done everything, in fact, but the ultimate. He wanted to have her pinioned under him, to hear her gasping reaction to his screwing. He was well aware that if he didn't have the outlet of

Mrs. Goldenbaum, he'd probably have raped Eve by now; it wasn't fair of her to tease him in this way.

His mind lingered on Mrs. Goldenbaum, on her nudity and what they would do together. It was a voluptuously pleasant thought and the images in his memory seemed hardly possible, now. He knew nothing about her. He didn't even know her Christian name... and yet that had happened between them.

He dozed off, slowly, picturing screwing Mrs. Goldenbaum, and in his dream she gradually became Eve.

CHAPTER TWELVE

The wall lights were low, giving a dark, velvet splendour to the room. At intervals the wall was adorned with old Flemish paintings, illuminated by a tiny strip of fluorescent light below each. Little bronze statuettes and a couple of marble busts had their places in the corners. The wallpaper was dark red and the curtains were leaf green. The heavy atmosphere of decadence just came off.

This room led into another through a Spanish archway and that room too was heavy and splendid like an over-ripe fruit. Where this one was red and green, the other was just blue. And beyond it was another in yellow. It was strangely impressive and Eve was impressed.

She was impressed, too, by the people who thronged these rooms, knocking back Scotch and champagne as if it was tea. She could only think that they glittered. They exuded a rich glitter—with their clothes, their jewels and their manners. They were not of the world she knew. They were money, money and more money, not ostentatiously but in a way that just quietly acknowledged itself, without shouting, but without shame.

This was the home of the Earl of Haverford and the people at the party were drawn from the top rung of the Arts and the top rung of the people who patronised them. Most of the people were much older than Eve and she felt a sense of inadequacy against them. Things that had taken her a long time to acquire—such as a slight familiarity with Chekhov, Ibsen, Strindberg and so on—they had grown up with, absorbing into the blood-stream every nuance not only of the world's theatre, but the world's literature and art together with a personal acquaintance with the currents of politics and current affairs and banking and motor cars and travel and... everything was known to them. Impossible to see how they could have learned so much in the years at their disposal. She would have thought there were limits to how much one would absorb in a given time. They had another thing in common. These who were not actually artists themselves in one field or another had a respect for those that were which transcended any admiration of knowledge and learning for its own sake. It was only the recognition of this that made her able to stay there and face this galaxy of concentrated experience.

"Ah—there's Sir George," James Harrod said. "Let's go and have a word with him."

Eve followed his glance and her heart jumped. Sir George Duncan in person—and that would mean that Lady Celia was somewhere near. He looked shorter than he did on the stage, and older. His face was a little overpowering with that large nose and those deep-set eyes with their heavy brows. Her heart fluttered as they moved through the drinking, chatting crowd towards him.

He saw them coming and smiled at James Harrod.

"Hello Jim. How's the novel coming on?"

"Frightened of it. Can't bear to think that when it finally gets down on the paper it won't amount to anything."

"Always run it as a serial in the *Daily Express* if it's no good."

James Harrod chuckled.

"There are some things even I won't do," he said.

Sir George looked expectantly at Eve. In fact he looked at her very expectantly so that she felt herself flush.

Harrod introduced them and Sir George seemed to stroke her hand as they shook them.

"What are you doing here with such a bunch of old fogies?" he asked.

"Old fogies!" Her words were an eloquent answer to his question.

"Well perhaps we have our points, eh James?" Sir George said.

He looked at Eve appraisingly. To her astonishment she saw he was stripping her with his eyes. For some reason it was the last thing she had expected. It reduced him to an easy, familiar level.

"You certainly *do* have your points," she heard herself saying. "When I see you and Lady Celia in *A View from the Bridge* I feel like giving up trying."

"Ah, flattery, flattery," said Sir George. "I'm never too old or famous to love it. So you're in the business, eh?"

Eve told him what she did and all the time she talked his eyes studied her, dropping to the prominent points of her breasts, measuring the slim waist, ranging over her features as if he were sizing her up for a portrait. She found this very personal interest highly exciting.

"Ah yes," he said. "I know the company. There are better ones, if you'll forgive my saying so, but of course there are so many of us, sadly so many of us." He grinned at Harrod. "There must be more people wanting to get on the stage even than there are others wanting to be drama critics, eh James?"

"Not quite," Harrod said. "There's a waiting list of ten thousand for my funeral. It becomes embarrassing with so many people enthusiastic for your ruin. Worse than being Prime Minister."

"What's the answer then, Jim. Wine, women or opium?"

"Whatever comes to hand," Harrod said, glancing obliquely at Eve. She had the feeling that they both wanted to take her off and debauch her.

A small, rather heavily made up woman joined them. She exuded an animal magnetism like perfume. Lady Celia! Eve felt that her system would never recover form the jolts of excitement it was getting today.

"Hello darling," she said to Sir George with a hint of sarcasm. "Searching out the talent?"

Eve smiled nervously, not knowing quite what to make of this approach.

"Finding it, my dear," Sir George retorted smoothly.

Lady Celia gave Eve a long, cool, soul-searching glance. She had the most flaming dark eyes Eve had ever seen. Eve felt that her innermost thoughts were revealed to this woman. She sensed that there was absolutely no point in trying to ingratiate oneself with her. She was the sort of person who liked very few people and made no bones about everyone knowing it.

"Has my husband made any indecent suggestions to you yet?" she asked.

James Harrod came to the rescue.

"He was waiting for you to arrive, Ce, so as not to have any advantage."

"It would be the first time he'd ever played it straight," she said, without humour.

The burning eyes roamed over Eve. There was no direct hostility in them, simply a cold, analytical penetration. Eve felt extremely uncomfortable. She didn't pretend to understand the turn the conversation had taken. Nobody remembered or bothered to introduce her to Lady Celia. Introductions had been bypassed.

"You're an actress, are you?" Lady Celia asked. "You have the look."

"In a small way," Eve said.

"Don't be modest, dear. It isn't becoming."

"I'm not concerned about being becoming," Eve heard herself say.

"Oh you should, dear. It's the only saving grace."

"I think treating other people like human beings is the only saving grace."

Harrod grinned. Sir George looked at his wife in amusement.

"How old fashioned, my dear," Lady Celia said, her eyes unyielding.

"Not at all," Harrod interrupted. "It all depends on how we think human beings should be treated. It leaves the question wide open for personal idiosyncracies."

Sir George chuckled.

"A good answer then, eh my dear?" he said to his wife. "I think we should invite her to the anniversary party, don't you?"

"By all means," Lady Celia said sweetly.

"Two hundredth performance of the show," Sir George said to Eve. "A little gathering *chez nous*. Will you come?"

"I'd love to," Eve said.

This seemed hardly to be the world of reality. This was the stuff that dreams were made of. And yet... she had the impression they expected something from her.

"Right," Sir George said. "The more the merrier. Jim here will tell you how to get there—next Sunday. We prefer the Sabbath for these dos."

Eve was making quick calculations. She could just about spare the fare. It would mean more excuses to Adam and Rushton, but that was a small matter. As it was Sunday she wouldn't have to pretend to fall ill as she had today to get the evening off.

"What's lined up for the future," James Harrod was asking them.

Eve hardly listened. She watched their lips moving, saw their eyes flicker back over her, but she didn't really take in any of the words. All you had to do was to move in the right circles. That was all there was to it. Amazing!

After a time they excused themselves and moved on and Harrod went to get them some more drinks.

"Want to have a look at the place?" he asked. "You know the flat across the landing belongs too."

They walked through the plush and gilt rooms, helping themselves to canapes on the way. She was enthusiastic about the Duncans.

"Oh they have some strange sides," Harrod said.

"How? What do you mean?"

"You'll find out."

He refused to discuss them further, but led her instead across the thick-carpetted landing from which the broad thick-carpetted stairways ran away to one side of the lift and into the suite of rooms beyond the open door opposite.

There were few people in this section of the flat, but there were trays of glasses and bottles everywhere and they helped themselves liberally. Some of the rooms were in darkness and it was through the big wooden doors of one of them that Harrod led her. He closed the door behind them and pulled her to him, breathing hard.

"Where are we?" she asked softly. "Somebody will come."

"It will only be me," he grinned. "This is one of the bedrooms. I know this place like the palm of my hand."

"But won't anybody come in?"

"Only for a screw. If they find it's occupied they'll leave. In any case they won't be able to see who we are."

He took her glass and she heard him put them down somewhere, though she could hardly see anything in the darkness.

He came back to her and his lips came moistly down on hers, drawing them into his mouth and then crushing them back against her teeth. She felt his teeth against hers and then his tongue probing between them.

"My god," he said. "I want you badly."

He pushed her back, gently, kissing her neck, and lowered her onto a bed.

"My dress," she whispered. "It'll be ruined."

"Take it off," he whispered back.

She took it off. She was trembling with excitement. The strangeness of the surroundings, the drink, the fact that someone might come and that that someone might even be Sir George or Lady Celia, those Olympian figures, thrilled and frightened her to the very core. She felt a thrilling desire to be naked, completely naked, on the silk coverlet she could now feel against her bare thighs and shoulders. She undid her brassiere. She heard rustlings in the darkness. He was undressing, too.

She undid her girdle, took off her briefs and kicked off her shoes. She lay back voluptuously on the silk coverlet, feeling like a royal favourite of centuries gone by. She felt her breasts tenderly with her own hands, and the soft firmness of her belly and thighs.

"What luxury," she whispered.

Harrod came down on her then, panting. The moment his flesh touched hers she quivered with sensual delight and he gritted out between his teeth: "My god, I'm going to fuck you as you've never been fucked before."

"Please, please," she whispered.

Their mouths locked together and she rubbed against him, stroking his hard cock with her slim fingers, drawing her nails gently over his testicles. He gasped a couple of times and his prick jerked up of its own volition away from her pursuing fingers.

His mouth moved on voraciously over her neck and shoulders and down to her hard, erect-nippled breasts. He sucked the nipples, bringing gasps of mixed pleasure and pain from her with his hard little bites. And then his mouth moved on away and he slid down her body. His lips were on her ribs, below the breasts, on her belly. His tongue explored her navel, briefly and moved away following the line of down straight down to the sudden protrusion of pubic hair. He slid his hands under her buttocks and lifted them slightly. She felt his tongue on her thighs. Her loins were a whirlpool. And suddenly his tongue had shot into her cunt, like a darting lizard, sending a sharp, quivering spasm up her spine.

"Oh, wonderful, wonderful," she breathed.

He licked and sucked, drawing the clitoris up to its full erect state, using lips and teeth and a fluid tongue. She wanted him inside her. She wanted her quim to be turned inside out and drubbed with his prick.

She pulled his hair gently, her eyes closed in ecstasy.

"Get inside me," she breathed. "Fuck me; fuck me to death."

The drink was making her slightly dizzy. The effect added to the illusion that she was just a personified quim, aching and longing. Nothing mattered in the world but sex. At this moment, nothing else mattered. Not the theatre, not Sir George, not fame, not riches. Only this lovely, swirling, exultantly dizzying nucleus of pleasure in her cunt which throbbed and pulsated under his attack.

He slithered up her, forcing her thighs wide. She was wet and wide open to him. Her cunt was like a redhot tunnel waiting for an ice-cold penis to come stinging in.

And it came, suddenly, smoothly, superbly, shatteringly. It came in at the beginning and soared right through to the end, bringing one long scream of ecstasy from her open mouth. And it began to move around inside her and in and out, never stopping, always probing, seeming to go farther all the time, as if it was eating at her heart.

She pinned back her legs, wriggling her buttocks on the slippery luxury of the silken coverlet. She was a mass of exquisite moisture between her thighs. Her loins blazed at her mind as if to overpower all thought, all being except themselves. She was vaguely aware of his hands running over her like flames, of his lips, of the hot friction of his body as he squirmed and swarmed against her.

She saw the flash of light as the door opened and somebody came in but she paid no attention and nor did he. Nothing mattered but this blaze of soul-raking passion which had caught them as if they were boiling together in a cauldron. He filled her, filled her utterly like a lost piece of herself. If only this could go on for ever, she could live and be happy for ever, wanting nothing else in this world.

She gasped out words at him between her streams of panting breath.

"Screw me, darling! Screw me for ever!... Wonderful, wonderful... Oh, up, up, up... Come high in me, darling..."

She panted and writhed. She heard his wailing breath. His penis was a huge, unrelenting animal, snuffling and hurtling into her, making her tingle from the tips of her toes to the back of her skull. It was a dream, a heavenly nightmare. To have such exquisite happiness in one's own power all the time, within one's own body, was unthinkably glorious. She was a goddess and he was a god—the goddess of cunt and the god of prick in a heavenly fuck. She screamed and gasped, on and on endlessly...

CHAPTER THIRTEEN

Adam was already high in the taxi which took them from the Dorchester to the party where he was to meet the kings of the art world. London was a glittering world of yellow lights shining on the leaves of trees in Park Lane, of commissionaires in brown and yellow, of stars high in a bright sky, of bits of blue and yellow neon and the flood of light from shopwindows; a glorious, warm and gold and silver fairyland.

They had just been locked in her suite for four hours. God, she'd made him work and now he was pleasantly exhausted. He'd had her in every position they could both think of. They'd rolled over and over on the bed in passion, over and over on the floor, spilling the bottles of champagne she'd ordered in the suite. They rubbed their naked bodies together, every separate inch of hers against every separate inch of his. He'd bent her over chairs, stood her on her head, rolled her in a ball. Had he done it? Or had she done it? He wasn't sure of anything now. They had just had an orgy. A real, wild orgy, dripping and groaning and slapping and scratching and clinging and thrusting and coming all over the place.

And then they had collapsed, lying side by side on a ruined bed, naked, just touching at the hips, in a sleep of the dead, from which they had been roused by the telephone call she'd asked to be made to let them know when it was nine o'clock.

"You're a lovely, handsome boy," she told him. And she kissed him tenderly on the tip of his hanging penis, gave his buttocks a gentle slap and said they must get ready to leave for the party.

They'd had a shower together, drunk a hair of the dog, dressed, and now they were cruising through the mystery of the metropolis with relaxed, surfeited bodies and minds.

He really began to like her. He'd certainly learned a lot from her. There was nothing the woman didn't know about sex. Once she'd sucked him off with a mouthful of hot water, without swallowing the water, a feat that he thought was near impossible and certainly one which had an excruciatingly gorgeous effect.

"I don't think his wife will be there," she said, as the taxi sped through the cool, elegant streets. "Which is a pity in a way, because she'd fall for you and influence him on your behalf. But on the other hand if you paid her any attention I'd be jealous, so perhaps it's just as well. Perhaps I'll offer him a quick go in return for your exhibition."

"How could you find the energy?" he asked with a lazy grin.

"Truth to tell I don't think I could," she said. "For the first time in my life I don't think I could. Now there's a compliment for you."

She pressed his hand.

"Don't you go wandering off with any other women, or I shan't help you at all," she warned. "I want another session in the morning when we'll be so full of wine that it'll be bursting our glands with sexuality."

Adam smiled. What a pity, he thought, that Eve couldn't know about this amazing double life of luxury he was leading. How envious she would be of the Dorchester and Park Lane and rich parties and millionaires. Perhaps once he'd won fame and riches he'd be able to buy her the role she wanted.

They reached the block of luxury flats where the party would now be well in progress. He paid the taxi with some of the money she'd given him ("It looks better if you pay") and they took the lift up to the fourth floor where a doorman was guarding the open doors which formed separate parts of the flat on each side of the landing.

"I hope the old bastard's turned up," she said softly as a servant took their coats.

They went through the entrance hall into the first of the rooms. It was dimly lit and the dark red walls gave off an air of decadent splendour.

Adam noticed the old paintings around the wall immediately. Old masterpieces, worth a fortune, which brought a whistle of admiration from his lips.

The place was thronged with guests and the drink and canapes looked like a royal wedding. The carpet was so thick it was like walking on a mattress to cross it.

The party was very well under way. In fact nobody appeared to notice their arrival; the time for formal reception had long since passed.

"Grab yourself a drink," Mrs. Goldenbaum said, "and we'll find Leon."

They pushed through the room, to an accompaniment of nods and smiles from various groups, until they reached the buffet. Adam looked in awe at the massive array of bottles and the huge variety of canapes: smoked salmon on toast, little Greek meat balls, miniature baclavas that turned out not to be baclavas at all, but to have meat in them.

"He's Greek—as you can see," Mrs. Goldenbaum said, referring to the host.

With their glasses filled with the best champagne—"Better not mix it too much," she'd warned—they moved back into the room searching for Leon Dalmain, the gallery owner.

They found him in the next room, standing alone, studying a visiting card which someone had just given him.

"Gracie, my dear—I didn't think you'd really get back from Paris, you know. Whoever wants to."

"There speaks a man who's never had permanent quarters there," Mrs. Goldenbaum said. "It's always nice to have a break, Leon. Makes the return so more tasty."

"I suppose you're right, darling. I must get myself a little place there some time. But I'll have to sell the house in Malaga to be able to afford it."

"You poor man."

Gracie Goldenbaum smiled solicitously and turned to Adam.

"I'd like you to meet a friend of mine—a very talented friend," she said, giving Adam a look which said that she regarded him as having more talents than one. Introductions were made and Mrs. Goldenbaum, after a little general conversation, launched herself on the object of the meeting to such good purpose than within half an hour Leon Dalmain, who respected her opinion, invited Adam to produce some paintings for him to see. Mrs. Goldenbaum invited him round to the Dorchester next day. With her usual optimistic gusto she'd seen to it that Adam had some of his work ready to view.

Leon Dalmain accepted with a grin. He turned to Adam.

"Well young man, when Grace Goldenbaum roots for someone so completely, I can only assume that he must have really enormous talent." He, too, placed an ambiguous emphasis on the word and smiled at Mrs. Goldenbaum.

"His talent," she assured him, "is prodigious."

They moved on through the party. Adam had a couple of short but memorable conversations with two artists of international stature. And, with the courage of drink, disagreed firmly with the opinion of an eminent art critic on the qualities of Berthe Morisot.

He and Grace Goldenbaum separated for periods, but she never left him long at any critical time, such as when his group might include an attractive woman, old and experienced enough to seduce him away.

Adam hardly noticed how often his glass was brimful of champagne. If the level dropped more than an inch somebody usually refilled it for him. On the few occasions that he managed to drink it down, another glass was always handy. The cumulative effect began to tell on him. His eyes grew heavy and his head a little dizzy.

"I have to lie down for a bit," he told her quietly as they met in a tour of the room. "I should hate to be sick all over this beautiful carpet."

"I must just wait and see Arthur Bryant," she said. "He's been promising for years to get a Chagall from Lord Edwards for me, but the noble lord hasn't been induced to part with it yet... Why don't you lie down in one of the bedrooms across the landing and I'll come and find you in half an hour."

"Yes," he agreed. "Best thing; I'll do that."

"Don't have any more drink," she said. "And don't get up to mischief. If any sex-starved old ladies come and tickle your secret weapon, just warn them I'll drop an atom bomb where it hurts most."

She led him to the door and showed him the open rooms across the landing.

"Don't worry about anything," she said. "They're quite bohemian in this establishment. You'll probably find some of the beds already occupied—just curl up at their feet."

Adam walked out onto the landing and into the rooms opposite. The first was illuminated, but rather more dimly than those from which he'd come. There were a few couples chatting quietly. It seemed the room in which business deals were furthered on the side, or perhaps a job was offered from one to another, or perhaps clandestine liaisons were worked out.

Adam hardly looked at them. He blundered through the room into the doorway of another in which there was no light except the path cut by the glow from the first. He opened a door at the end. The next room was not a bedroom. He considered curling up on the floor, but desire for greater comfort drove him on through another door which he opened and then closed after him as the trace of light, filtering through from way back, showed him that this was what he sought.

With a sigh of relief he stumbled to the bed whose vague outline he'd seen and rolled onto it, a blissful smile covering his face as he felt the soft give and the cool silk of the coverlet under him. The fact of lying down, relaxed, cleared his mind a little. It had been clouded by pure nervousness that he was going to find nowhere to be alone and in the comfortable dark.

A continuous noise filtered through to him. It was very close. He closed his eyes, opened them again and strained to see into the darkness, gave up, thinking What the hell does it matter? and rolled over onto his back.

With both ears now clear, he heard the sound more distinctly, a soft, but penetrating gasping on two levels, one high, one low. He kept absolutely still, his flesh creeping.

He listened to the gasping. It was somebody. It was somebody in pain. He lay motionless, holding his breath, wondering what he should do. And then he heard a female murmur, a sound of quiet exclamations and then a male obscenity. He relaxed and laughed convulsively inside. It was a couple making love. My god, he thought, they must be really at it not to have noticed me come in, not to have cared.

They were very close, presumably on an adjacent bed. He could make out the rustling of the bedclothes. He even imagined he could hear the friction of their labouring bodies. And the gasps and moans rose and fell in the quiet room.

He began to grow quite excited. He wished he could see them. Were they naked? Or did she simply have her dress up over her thighs and was he simply thrusting out through his open flies?

The girl's voice was giving little shrieks. My god, he thought, what a shag she sounds like. He imagined her young. The gasps sounded young and the murmur, so passionate, of the voice sounded young. That's what I really need, he thought, a beautiful young girl rather than this elderly sex maniac I'm stuck with. He thought of Eve and his heart and loins filled with longing. He found he had an erection and his hand moved down to his loins and fondled it.

Now he heard the girl murmuring words, words broken and swallowed and spat with her passion, so that he thought he would die if he didn't have a girl like that.

"Darling... deep, deep... hard... oh wonderful..."

He listened with aching, strained ears for every nuance and it suddenly seemed to him that there was something familiar about the voice, but he dismissed the idea.

He almost dozed off to the verbal accompaniment of their passion. It would fill his ears and swamp him, that pleasure and pain that came from them. And then he would come back to full consciousness with a start and stare over into the darkness, aware that he could probably reach out, lean a bit and touch their bodies.

He heard the bed creaking and groaning under their furious movement. He could hardly distinguish their groans and explosions of breath.

He heard the girl's voice say: "I'm coming... coming..." and then croon off into a weird little wail as she choked and spluttered.

Adam's body was tense, his throat parched and a furious aching desire expanded his lungs to breaking point. He considered going to find Grace Goldenbaum and dragging her in here with him to get relief from his pent-up sexuality, but he couldn't tear himself away from the fascinating eavesdropping for a minute.

He heard the girl sigh deeply and then give occasional cries as if of surprise or pain when, presumably, her partner shoved his prick a little deeper than before.

Now the man's cry was growing and he began to mutter commands to the girl to excite himself as his orgasm approached.

"Spread them wider... open... open... I'll split your belly..."

Adam heard these oaths with a flushed and haunted desire. His curiosity about them was overwhelming.

How he envied them their fury, the man the enthusiasm of the girl who was his cushion.

Adam's prick was standing up on end, bursting through his pants, or trying to. It felt hot and razor sharp inside with feeling. He felt that shortly he might come in his trousers.

He listened to the humping fury of the man, belabouring the now satisfied girl. He pictured him pushing her legs up to her shoulders to get farther in. He heard her responding squeals begin to jerk from her lips once more. He felt he wouldn't be able to bear the male climax; it would be too much torture for his own aching body.

But when it finally came, he lay quiet, his eyes wide, his limbs aching with the tension in which he'd held them.

Gasp after gasp after gasp came from the unseen lips in wave after passionate wave until it seemed to him that the man must be a reservoir of sperm. And then it finally simmered away and there was a final, luxurious gasp and then silence except for a strong panting and little post-act moans from the girl.

They lay still for a long time with only an occasional murmur and Adam, listening for anything there was to hear, finally began to grow drowsy again and almost forget they were there.

In fact he did doze off, but he became alert again with the rustling of the nearby bedclothes. He listened to a fresh murmuring and then the girl gave another voluptuous intake of breath and cried "Oh darling!"

They were at it again. That hadn't taken long. He felt again there was something familiar about the voice, but he couldn't imagine what it could possibly be.

The male voice whispered: "Who taught you to make love like that?"

The answer was a gasp and an exclamation of: "Oh, do that again; it's beautiful!"

A wild thought flashed through Adam's mind. It flushed him in a quick, nervous spasm. He lay with all his senses alert. But he couldn't take in the idea. It was ridiculous. He listened to the gulps and groans and occasional sucking noises of their lovemaking and grinned nervously to himself for having such a ridiculous idea. He wished he could relate his thought to Eve. It would fill her with mirth if he could isolate the fact that he thought he'd come across her making love with a stranger in a dark bedroom, from admission of his own activities.

His penis, which had deflated, began to elongate again. He had to find relief somehow.

The girl's voice said, broken by little gasps: "This is so wonderful—nobody's done it to me so marvellously before."

Adam froze. It *was* Eve! While his mind denied the possibility, his instincts told him there could be no doubt. That was her voice, broken and racked with the passion of being dominated and fucked by some strange man. It *couldn't* be. There were millions of voices like that. No, there weren't; there was only one and there was no doubt about it. He was having hallucinations—probably asleep. His thoughts see-sawed and leapfrogged and fell one against the other in utter confusion. There was only one way to find out. But it was just *too* ridiculous. Why, Eve was at home, learning her next role. And in any case Eve wouldn't fuck. And in any case... The arguments against what his ears had told him were overwhelming.

He relaxed uncomfortably. In any case the girl had spoken like a whore. He relaxed a little more. Impossible!

Their sobs and heart-rending, genital-rending, animal noises, had continued unabated, unconcerned for the drama they had awakened in the unknown listener's mind.

"Yes, yes," the man's voice grunted, "stick your finger up me..."

"Let me put my legs over your shoulders," the girl groaned.

Adam turned cold. He rolled off the bed, shaking, and fumbled around the walls. His head throbbed. He couldn't find one—and all the time their intertwining sounds of sex went on. He reached frantically around the floor, found a wire and followed it with his hands. It led to a lamp on a small table. He switched it on and turned in the sudden glare to the noise of the coupling. His jaw clamped and something in his head blazed as if a glinting spear had slashed through it.

Eve's startled face turned towards him and a man's face looked over in bewilderment. She was naked, utterly naked, spreadeagled under him with her thighs pulled back at a sharp angle. Even in the split second before he moved towards them, Adam saw the way the man's rigid cock disappeared into the crack between her thighs, so that only a tiny little stretch of it was showing, wet and glistening.

Eve was too horrified to speak. But then she yelled as Adam launched himself at them.

James Harrod scrambled out of her and met Adam's drunken rush with a desperate straight right, which made his head spin but didn't stop his momentum.

The three of them sprawled on the bed in a flail of arms and legs and heaving bodies. Adam lashed out at Eve's face, but his hand only caught her juicy rump as she slithered away. Harrod caught him round the neck and they fell together, rolling over and over on the floor.

Adam kicked out and felt his shoe crash into flesh, a fist hit him on the side of the face and he lashed back, feeling a nose splay. He followed that up, rising to his feet with another blow which caught Harrod on the neck. Harrod, also rising, fell backward and his foot caught Adam in the groin.

Adam rolled over backwards. His head hit something sharp and hard and the world dissolved in a dizzying, light-streaked blackness.

CHAPTER FOURTEEN

In Adam's dream, he was visiting a brothel. He went up the stairs and entered a room where the prize prostitute awaited him on a bed. She was Eve. She had Eve's face and Eve's body, but she was a stranger to him. She didn't recognise him, only confronted him with a look which was half quizzical, half voluptuous. There was a remoteness under the invitation in her eyes. The communication was aloof, under the pretence of interest. It was like being in a big city that you felt you should know and yet you found no friends in it, no doors open to you, no friendliness, nothing with which you could feel at home.

The scene changed and now he was looking down through the window at the same Eve. She looked passionate now, as if she were lost in a green, tropical, orchid world of ecstasy that was beyond him, that he had never dreamed of in his weirdest dreams. She was a thousand years old and he was in his adolescence. She was a thousand years old and she had the body of a beautiful girl and she lay on a bed and men came to her. He tried to move but it was impossible. He was embedded in concrete. He tried to turn his eyes away, but they would not turn, to close them, but they would not close. And he watched the men come to her through mists which accentuated their strangeness. They were nobody he knew. He could not believe in them. Except when their naked bodies flowed over and settled onto Eve and they began that dance of love in which she languidly joined. He watched the langour change to a ferocity that belonged to the jungle with wild animals that roamed and spat and lashed out with inch-long claws and drew back their lips on sabre teeth.

He saw the men drift away and others come. He saw the hundred and one things that happened between them. There was nothing they didn't do to one another. And at the end of each Eve smiled and stretched out like a satisfied cat and her eyes opened and looked up at him with that strange, remote, hard, indifferent look that saw in him only some accomplice spirit.

He cried out and tried to struggle. He wanted to smash the face that smiled up at him with that disgusting mixture of innocence and craft. But he couldn't move. He couldn't move a muscle of his body except his jaws.

Without being able to see, he suddenly realised that, in fact, he had no body; there was nothing to him below the face in which all hatred was concentrated. He was a statue, nothing but a statue. He was ceasing to exist... ceasing to exist... and all the while the face below stared up at him with an awful, knowing grin.

He awoke, crying out and sweating and frightened and empty deep inside.

Mrs. Goldenbaum was sitting beside the bed in the Dorchester suite, the picture of concern. She was holding a glass of water and she had a soft sponge in her other hand.

"Easy... easy..." she said. "You're all right, my sweetheart."

He came back to normal fairly quickly, gazing around in surprise.

"What happened?" he asked, knowing that something strange had taken place. "What happened?"

"Relax, relax, my silly boy," she said gently. "Next time your champagne is going to be severely rationed so that you don't get into any silly fights with drama critics over the way Ibsen should be played."

CHAPTER FIFTEEN

It was a dark night with a high breeze which sent the clouds scudding across the moon from blackness to sudden washes of smoky white. The trees and bushes on the stretch of Common stood out like old black gallows with bodies flapping and swaying from them, lit up every few minutes by the sudden appearance of the moon and then plunged again into a darkness which reduced them to ghoulish outlines towering above the heath.

Eve glanced around her apprehensively as she crossed the waste. She had been relying on Rushton giving her a lift to within a short distance of her home, but his wife had arrived unexpectedly at the theatre after the performance and she had had to make the journey across the stretch of Common alone. She didn't know quite what she was apprehensive about—it was true of course that there were so many assaults on girls and young women and even elderly women by rape-rob-and-run sex maniacs. But there was no history of that sort of thing on this Common. After all, the area was a good-class one where that sort of thing didn't happen. Everyone was too well balanced. She tittered to herself at the thought. Nonetheless... and she sobered up... there was always a first time, and there was something very eerie about this particular night.

She forced herself to think about pleasant things to take her mind off her surroundings and she pictured the coming Sunday when she was going to visit Lord and Lady Duncan at their country home. She went over in her mind the way to get there. Harrod had given her full details. He had another engagement.

She thought of Harrod and that took her mind back to the shattering scene in which Adam had discovered them at the party. To think of it now made her blood run cold. She just hadn't seen Adam since. He'd made no attempt to contact her nor she him. It was finished between them, of course; impossible after that. In any case, her mind was on the future, which glittered with a glamour in which Adam had no place. She found herself trying very hard to convince herself that this was so. But somewhere deep down inside her she felt the shadowy presence of a great aching regret. Adam. Adam. She whispered his name to herself.

She had no idea what had happened to him. She had run into another dark room to dress while they fought. There, drama within drama—and she smiled to herself at how incredible it all was—she had had to fight off the lecherous hands of some elderly man who'd said he was the Count of Mons. He'd caught her naked, she'd run right into him. And what a struggle that had been, with his leathery hand mauling all over her, until the stinging fury of her nails had finally convinced him that he'd better lay off. And then Harrod, fully dressed, had come to find her and then they'd bumped into that sinewy Jewish woman as they looked back into the bedroom and she'd shouted at them: What had they done to Adam, who was lying unconscious on the floor? Harrod had told her that calm story about a disagreement they'd had about producing Ibsen and the ensuing fight. Adam was all right, just banged his head a bit.

Then they'd left, with the woman fussing towards Adam behind them. Eve had felt torn between her desire to get away and her desire to see that Adam was really all right. There had really been nothing for it. She had gone home with Harrod and they'd made love and love again throughout the night, until in the morning they were sick of the sight of each other. No, that was an exaggeration, she told herself. But for comparative strangers they'd had rather a lot of extreme intimacy all in one lump. She'd promised to ring him after the Duncan's party. There were several books he said she ought to read, but she hadn't wanted to take them away with her that morning.

Life was getting rather complicated, she told herself. Excuses to her mother, to her aunt, to Adam, to Rushton. There was no end to it.

She gave a start. There was a movement near her. Her heart began to thump furiously and she stared into the darkness, increasing her pace. She could see nobody. It must have been a movement of the wind in the shrubbery. She quickened her pace. The quicker she was off the Common and under the lights of the lane where she lived, the better she'd be pleased.

She sensed the movement again. It was something more than the breeze. It contained a menace which was difficult to define. But she was still not sure if it was the ever-lurking menace of her own imagination.

Again it happened. There was somebody following her, moving alongside her, half screened by the bushes. Her heart leapt up into her mouth. She glanced around. The lights of the town behind her were distant, those of the built up area ahead not yet in view. She refused to run. Never let them see you're afraid. In any case, she told herself desperately, it may be someone exercising his dog.

And then a figure sprang through the bushes towards her. She opened her mouth, but was too paralysed with fright to scream. And then she saw it was Adam.

"Adam, my god!" she burst out. "What a fright you gave me."

But she was still frightened. Why had he stalked her across the waste like this? Why this spot for a confrontation—the first since the night of the party?

He came towards her without speaking. She stood her ground, the backs of her knees sweating.

"Adam," she said, "I was going to ring you."

The words sounded pathetically hollow and false, like a feeble, crooked arm raised to fend off a blow.

He stopped close to her and looked at her. His face was contorted and his eyes looked bloodshot and more ruthless than she'd seen them. He smelt of drink, but there was something terribly sober about him.

"Adam," she said. "Come home and have a coffee. I wanted to see you."

Still he didn't speak, just stood gazing at her face with a hard, snarling expression, as if he hated her to the very marrow.

"Why don't you speak?" she cried sharply. And then coaxingly: "Let's got home and have a talk. Mother will have gone to bed."

"You vile bitch!"

He spat the words so fiercely she imagined them hurtling wetly into her face. And then he stepped forward and caught her by the shoulders, holding his face within an inch or two of hers.

"How many others have fucked you?" he snarled.

"You virgin! You pure, frightened creature! What had you got against me, you filthy rotten bitch. You whore, whore, whore!"

He pulled her to him and slammed his mouth on hers. But there was such a hostile savagery in his manner even of the kiss, that she pulled away from him instinctively, frightened. He slapped her then, his face hard and vicious. The blow lashed across her face, so hard that it knocked her sideways. She was so frightened that she hardly felt it and she turned to run.

He caught her before she'd taken two steps and twisted her round. His second slap caught her higher up on the side of the head, jolting her neck.

"No Adam, please... don't be silly... we can talk..."

He hit her again so that her face stung cold with the blow. He caught her by the neck. She struggled, fighting and pleading at the same time. They fell to the ground and he sat astride her, lashing her face from side to side until she was almost insensible and hardly knew whether she was on the way to dying. He began to tear at her clothes wildly, ripping and tearing them off her. She tried to get up but he knocked her back. She struggled with him, vaguely aware she was in her underclothes and then that her stockings were round her ankles and that her brassiere straps had broken and that he had ripped her knickers away.

"Adam, Adam," she managed to sob. "Have mercy... you'll kill me."

But all the time he didn't speak. He slashed her breasts with his hands. He pulled a whippy stick from the bushes at his hands and lashed her across the belly with it so that she writhed away in pain and rolled over onto her smarting stomach. He pinioned her and whipped her buttocks, her back, her thighs, with the thin, swishing cane. And then he rolled her over and, in the midst of the pain, she found her legs forced brutally apart and his prick pushed nastily into her unready quim.

She began to cry, completely breaking down, but, firmly inserted in her, he began to fuck her savagely, intending to hurt, scraping his penis along the walls of her vagina, bending her thighs back to her shoulders, coming right out of her and then thrusting right up to the cervix in a thunderous jab so that she choked with the sudden agony and humiliation.

"Adam, no... not like this... no, no... it hurts Adam..."

But he ignored her, panting, snarling into her face, twisting her body like a rubber shape so that he could fill the increasing breadth of her hole. He seemed to go so high up in her that at the zenith of every stroke a little pain stabbed her loins as if he were breaking into some delicate inner tube.

"It's just another fuck," he snarled, breaking silence at last. "Just another shag like the scores you've had already."

"It's not true Adam... oh, Adam, stop..." she pleaded, hardly knowing what she was saying.

His hand smashed across her mouth, bruising the lips and he dug his fingers cruelly hard into her breasts. She wanted to faint, but couldn't, aware all the time that he was forcing her into a back-aching position and that his every thrust was a physical semi-sweet agony, a mental horror because of the hate that drove it. This, in the wild confusion of her thoughts, she realised, was rape. She'd always thought it couldn't hurt really, but she'd never understood the hate that made it unbearable.

He began to go wild with passion and disgust at the same time. He twisted her body, worried it like a wild bull as he fucked. She felt the wet grass and the branches and the heat of the lashes and the cold blear of her tears. His hands pinched and pummelled her and she twisted unavailingly away from them. She saw his face above her a great mask of hatred, as his cock filled her finally like a stake that was impaling her slowly to death and then his face crumpled into a snarling, mouthing mess as he shot all the venom of his pent-up loathing into her quim...

He got up and left her soon afterwards with the weary, disgusted words: "You're just a cunt and a whore—and you'll be treated like a whore. I hope you choke with it!"

And then he had gone.

Eve lay exactly where he'd left her for some minutes. Not caring if anybody came by, her legs wide apart with the raw crevice open and her lashed body naked to the passing moon. If anyone else had sprung out and begun to screw her she wouldn't have bothered to resist. This was the lowest ebb—guilt, disgust, humiliation, misery and a sense of powerlessness which sprang from her complete inability to fight him off when it had really come to the underlying law of the jungle—strongest to survive. Except that she was still alive, after all. She pulled her limbs achingly together. There was mud and moss on her nude body and marks on her breasts and her belly. She winced at a dozen pains all over her and her passage felt so bruised and shaken that it seemed it must be coming to pieces.

She sat for further minutes, gently touching the weals on her breasts. She felt no anger against Adam yet; she was still a little dazed by it all.

She reached around for her bedraggled clothing. She hung the brassiere over her shoulders and put the torn briefs in the pocket of her coat which was screwed up beside her. She pulled her laddered stockings up her legs, noticing how cold her flesh was now, and then she put on her skirt and then the jumper. She forced herself to be composed. She stood up. Her body was shaken and her limbs trembled slightly as if she'd been on a blind the night before and felt very fragile. Standing there, crumpled, painful and disheveled, she felt the loneliness of herself well up inside her. A girl raped and beaten on a heath, with nobody to defend her. It was cold and sordid.

She began to walk awkwardly towards home, wiping her face with a handkerchief and combing her hair. Under the first lights she came to she made up her face, covering the bruise on her lips and blinking against the red rims of her eyes. She brushed herself down and prepared to sneak in quietly so as not to wake her mother. By the morning she'd be all right. A good rest without thinking was what she needed. To go out like a felled ox.

And, she reminded herself, with a surge of anger against the world, tomorrow she'd make Rushton buy her some new clothes.

CHAPTER SIXTEEN

Several of Adam's pictures were lined against the wall opposite. He and Leon Dalmain stood surveying them in the latter's Hampstead flat. Dalmain was being strangely non-committal, although it was obvious he was interested. There seemed no reason why he shouldn't have given a definite answer the week before at Mrs. Goldenbaum's suite in the Morchester.

"Hmmm," he said, rubbing his nose, thoughtfully. "Of course, nobody does anything for nothing these days you know," and added, "And they never did, come to think of it."

Adam didn't answer, not knowing what he was expected to say.

"Well, let's go back and have a drink with the family," Dalmain said.

Adam didn't mind that at all. Dalmain and his wife—a charming, gentle woman of about 50—had two quite beautiful daughters of 17 and 18. These two, Emily and Catherine, were dark, long-haired beauties, giving off a strange, rather voluptuous atmosphere of the Victorian beauties of old prints—full flowing curves, a rather secretive, withdrawn manner which was oddly suggestive of passion waiting for an opportunity to burst from them like sudden perspiration.

The family seemed to hang together as a group; the girls did not get on with their own activities. They indulged in strange pastimes, like combing their mother's hair and curling at their father's feet as he sat and talked, listening and smiling at Adam. There was something not quite normal about them but they were certainly handsome and that was enough for Adam to enjoy their presence.

He and Leon Dalmain wandered back into the room where they all were now and they all stopped what they were doing to smile and concentrate their attention on the newcomers.

"I think we'll have another drink, Joanna," he said to his wife. "Not the usual, the special one."

His wife smiled.

"Yes dear."

She disappeared and came back with a decanter filled with a reddish brown liquid, which she placed on a sideboard, and then arranged glasses.

"This is a specially potent drink," Leon Dalmain said. "Goes to the head and to the genitals with equal potency."

Adam was startled by his expression, but nobody else gave a hint of recognition, so he smiled politely. He'd already had a Scotch and felt in the mood for more.

"What is it?" he asked.

"Ah, that is a family secret," Dalmain told him, putting a slight emphasis on the word "family."

"Well give me some idea," Adam insisted.

"Well," Dalmain said. "It has many of the drinks you've heard of and some you haven't." And that was all he would say.

Joanna Dalmain poured five tumblers half full and handed them round. Adam was surprised to see that both the girls were permitted to quaff this supposedly potent drink which was, according to their father, a powerful aphrodisiac.

Dalmain raised his glass.

"Here's to quick stiff pricks and cannibal cunts," he said.

Adam stared at him in amazement, turning brick-red.

The others solemnly raised their glasses with murmurs of approval and took long draughts.

Purely to hide his embarrassment, Adam buried his face in his glass, taking a long, long swig. The liquid was firewater. It seemed to turn his whole body pink as if he'd broken out in a rash. It burned his throat too, a strange-tasting mixture with a nondescript parentage. He thought perhaps Scotch was the dominating ingredient, but then it seemed it might be vodka, or perhaps some strange rough wine or cider. But there were hints of other flavours he couldn't account for at all.

The effect was very quick. He felt different within twenty seconds and by the time he'd stopped thinking about the taste, he felt strangely light-headed, as if he were likely to take off to the ceiling.

"Good, eh?" Dalmain said, eyeing him curiously.

"What *is* it?" Adam insisted, feeling the effect creeping all over him, stronger every second. He looked around at the others. They were all watching him, the daughters with their lips slightly parted and gleaming desireful smiles on their faces. The wife slowly put her hand down on her thigh, watching him, and began to rub it gently as if it itched.

"Let us call it a witches' brew," Dalmain said. "A brew for Walpurgis night."

He held the bottle towards Adam and Adam, as if it were beyond his control, held out his glass and had it refilled. Dalmain smiled approvingly. He refilled the others' glasses and they all raised them together.

"Here's to fuck," Dalmain announced.

"And to suck," Emily said.

"To fucking in the ass," Catherine declared.

"To our guest," Joanna Dalmain toasted, with a meaningful stare at Adam.

They all looked at Adam, who no longer felt embarrassed. It was hilarious, he thought: these charming Victorian daughters, this gentle mother, this eminent father. And it was oddly exhilarating, as if all inhibitions were slipping away.

"To Walpurgis brew that makes all things possible," he said.

They all laughed and the daughters gave little claps in delight.

"I can see you catch on fast," Dalmain said.

They were all high. He refilled the glasses.

"We," he announced to Adam, "are members of the British Society of Witches. We worship the devil, we love so-called vice. Sex, in particular orgy, is our favourite pastime. You may have read of our procedure in one of the national Sunday newspapers—a mass-circulation organ for the masses Its particular gimmick is to give sex and 'vice' to its public under the guise of moralistic condemnation—a sickening newspaper, with cynical, nauseating young men working on it. One of their number got on to one of our newer members—a shorthand typist from Hendon, as a matter of fact—and she spilled the beans to him as if quite unaware of the furore she might create. He managed to get himself to one of our little festivals—a branch of us, that is—nobody well known fortunately—and watched our rites, which are pagan dances in the nude, minor beatings with switches and copulation. He was, apparently, so sickened by this spectacle that he wrote a slushy-mushy article about 'evil men and women' and 'vile rituals' which I'm told increased that week's circulation by rather more than half a million. He did not of course produce this masterpiece of cant and hypocrisy before he'd joined in for long enough to taste the delights of shagging our most voluptuous member and tried to date another in his room for a week later—telling her, if you please, to bring a pessary if she had one as he couldn't stand using contraceptives. The world is made of hypocrisy, of course; morality built on subconscious envy. Seduce a virtuous woman and you'll find she changes her view about ostracising fornicators. Screw her in the anus and you'll see she ceases to regard it as a vile habit indulged in by perverts. Make her suck you off and she'll no longer regard that as a disgusting aberration of Continental whores, und so weiter, und so weiter..."

Dalmain paused for breath, while Adam listened, fascinated not only by the words, but by the significance of this spiel. He looked at the daughters, glowing and alight with desire and he began to understand what was in store for him and it filled him with an ecstasy in glorious Technicolor. The daughters wriggled a little on their buttocks as if the words had began to make them feel too sexy to keep still. Adam knocked back the rest of his brew.

"Better take it easy," Dalmain said. "It's against the rules to pass out... As I was saying, we have these rites which we indulge in at varying times all over the country. There are many branches and sometimes one will exchange all its women with those of another branch to add a little zest. Joanna here has been screwed and sodomised by several hundreds I suppose in our time as witches. My daughters, however, are novices, not virgins, not in any of their passages, but novices, you understand. There are things they still don't know, pricks that could still frighten them... Now every so often we are expected to make a convert, doesn't matter which sex. Now, to come to the point, your painting is very good. Left to its own devices it might still make you famous—or it might never find the light of day other than that which filters through your studio window. Exhibited by me, however, it might not make you famous overnight—or it might—but, in any case it wall pass your name around and will certainly ensure some good purchases on the spot. Only the best people come to exhibitions in my gallery, the best, the richest and so on. From them, the fashion in painters radiates downwards..."

He filled Adam's glass a third full and gave a drop more to each of his family. Joanna Dalmain had now pulled her knees up under her chin with her feet on her chair. Adam could see the whole of the undersides of her thighs and her hairy quim, as he was obviously intended to since she wore no knickers and simply smiled at him when she saw his eyes drop down to the spot between her buttocks. He remained gazing at it in fascination while Dalmain went on talking.

"...so I have a bargain to make with you. I'll exhibit your work, if you'll exhibit yourself and join with us in the devil's rites from now on. Become, in short, a witch."

What an offer, Adam thought. Seldom had such an unnecessary bargain been struck. He would have paid them all he possessed to get at either of those daughters, or the mother for that matter. In fact, he could see how excited she was from the moisture on her pelvis and she was certainly no crone.

"I accept with pleasure," he said.

"Good," Dalmain said. "Right, everyone. Walpurgis night!"

They all stood up and begain to take off their clothes. Adam watched them. The mother was stripped first. She had been wearing nothing under her skirt and jumper. He pictured the "hundreds of men who'd screwed and sodomised" her as he looked at her strong, full, generous body and her smile, which was like an open cunt beckoning to him.

He tore his gaze away and looked at the daughters. They too disrobed rapidly. A quick striptease in which first one and then another part of their lovely, soft young bodies were uncovered. Finally naked, they twirled joyously in front of his gaze. Adam felt likely to have an orgasm down his trouser leg. Their youthful bodies were firmly curved with full breasts hard as large cooking apples, nicely rounded bellies like a Renoir painting and dimpled spheres of buttocks which looked soft as down. Their pubic hair was slight and silky and their little mounds jutted from between their moon-white thighs.

"Come on," Dalmain said. "This is a mixed party."

He was in the act of peeling off his underpants. Adam stared at him, too, fascinated. He had an unexpectedly bulky, muscular body covered in black hair which began at his chest and ran halfway down his thighs with his penis sticking out like a great lighthouse in a rough sea from the middle. One of his daughters, Emily, played with the tip of his prick absently while she watched Adam with a smile.

They were all looking at him, waiting for him to join them. Adam knocked back the last of the devil's potion, feeling it rage like hell-fire through his innards, and began to strip.

The air on his skin hit him like a douche of cold water. His prick was hot and moist with sweat, all his genital area was sweating profusely. He threw his clothes over a chair. Joanna, the wife, came over to him, smiling deeply. She didn't touch his prick. She poked her index finger up his ass, squirming it in to the first and then to the second knuckle joint. Adam was astonished at the extremely erotic effect this had on him. She moved her finger around in his bum and he let his mouth fall on the pointed nipples which reached out at him.

"That's enough," Dalmain shouted. "First things first. We must have order."

Mrs. Dalmain took her finger out of Adam's rectum. He contracted his ass over its tip, loath to let it escape, and then she gave his penis a gentle stroke and smiled at him as if to say they had plenty of time.

They formed in a circle and, on a sign from Dalmain, began to dance round one behind the other in a strange weaving dance that was half South American, half Indian. Moving behind Catherine, the elder of the two daughters, Adam felt his prick straining out to reach her. Her rump rotated provocatively, each buttock moving separately, hollowing into a dimple, rounding out again like a bubble. Her slim shoulders shook in a ripple which shivered down her smooth, tight-skinned back and ended at her nipped-in waist. He saw the muscles in her thighs, long and slender, protruding in long, fascinating ridges and then disappearing. His prick rode up almost against his belly, almost vertical with his desire. Beyond her he saw the younger one, Catherine, looking just that little, softer and more vulnerable. He had a profile view of her cheeky, upturned breasts and the s-shape in which her bottom stuck out behind her, waving like a little, fleshy signal to come right in. Dalmain led them, with his ramrod out like a buffer to clear the way of any obstruction, and Joanna Dalmain brought up the rear, occasionally letting her fingers wisp over Adam's buttocks or tickle very gently down his back.

Adam swayed his hips like the rest of them and undulated his buttocks. The very movement made him feel all the more sexy. His penis, with the foreskin tight back, stood out like a red-hot torch with its end burning with a strange pink light.

They all followed Dalmain, the drink in them goading them on to greater excesses of movement. Catherine began to lunge her ass backwards and downwards in sudden squatting movements and to jump flat-footed like an African warrior. Adam wanted to throw himself on her and feel that warm, beautifully-moulded density of flesh against him, but he controlled himself, maintaining the pattern which they were evidently to follow.

Without pausing in his body movements, Dalmain brought the party to a mark-time while he pulled a series of switches out of an old chest against one wall. They were like the heads of witches' broomsticks, except that instead of being made of rough twigs, they were composed of a thin, willowy, synthetic substance. Dalmain tossed them back, one each, and led off on the dance again.

Adam didn't know quite what to do with his switch until he suddenly felt a soft, many-fingered, titillating blow across his behind. It stung just a little, just enough to jerk his erection up in a quick arc. And then it came again, jerking him up once again as if he'd had a sudden injection in his cock.

He saw the same thing happening in front of him so he gave Catherine a good swish across the buttocks, delighted at the sexy way she squirmed in response. He began to lash her with the switch, across, between, over, under her buttocks, while they all weaved and swayed and squirmed their way around the room like a quintet of blind, wriggling worms.

Suddenly Dalmain gave a shout, whereupon Emily turned her back quickly to him, touched her toes, spread her legs apart, reached behind her with her hands and pulled apart her buttocks like a stage curtain, displaying a sweet little anus which stretched open like a fish's mouth as they watched and had obviously been well used. Dalmain waited until she was in position and then made a rush at her, ramming his prick straight home at the same time as he grabbed her hips to prevent her from falling over. He began to sodomise her hard and fast while she continued a strange, swaying dance from her hips, as if her torso had nothing to do with the part of her he was having.

Adam watched in an agony of discomfort and unsatisfied desire. They all watched for long enough to bring them to a state of sexual constriction even more intense than they'd felt during the dance, and then Catherine turned towards him, dropped to her knees and began to suck him with her full lips and hot, little mouth with its cool, glossy tongue. Joanna Dalmain came up behind them and guided them over to a divan. She pushed Adam down on it on his side and Catherine, who hadn't once released his throbbing rod, dropped down beside it, sucking. Joanna Dalmain then knelt over in front of his head beside the divan with her back towards him and pushed her wide-open cunt at his face. Adam took the cue and began to suck the soft, wet flesh of her vaginal lips. At the same time, Emily, still with her father bumming her like mad, moved over behind the divan and pushed two fingers up Adam's ass and began to saw away like a homosexual who'd abstained for forty days and nights.

They were a knot of wriggled, gasping bodies, a many-headed, many-legged, many armed monster with five voracious sexual organs.

Adam licked and bit the lips of Joanna Dalmain's quim, pushing his tongue up the crevice which she pushed down hard at his face. His mouth and nose and even his eyes were lost in a morass of glutinous flesh beyond which a body heaved and a mouth gasped encouragement. Catherine meanwhile sucked and pulled with moaning enjoyment at his raw, expanding cock. Behind him his ears were filled with the bellow of Dalmain's thunderous passion as he sodomised his daughter. And this sensation came vicariously to Adam through her twisting fingers, like a searching prick in his ass, enlarging his anus and giving him a little quiver of feeling in that vulnerable aperture.

He heard Dalmain come first in a great soul-rending cry and he must have barraged his prick so far up his daughter's hole that she gave a squeal of pain and pulled her fingers out of Adam's ass in a convulsive flick of her hand.

As if this were her cue, Catherine suddenly stopped sucking Adam's penis, pushed him over on his back and leapt astride him. She poised herself above his stiff tower and then, with a sharp lunge and a wild dervish howl, plunged her loins down on him so that she rode down his prick, enclosing it in the soft channel of her cunt like a dark tunnel with an express train racing through it. She let out another howl and began to dance and heave her hips about on his belly, screwing and squirming and gnashing her teeth.

Joanna Dalmain, who had been left in the cold, bent over her ass presented to Adam's profile, sprang into action and leapt astride his face to begin the grinding of her vagina in his mouth all over again.

As Catherine's tight quim rubbed up and down, up and down on Adam's weapon and he became more and more excited, so he sucked and bit more voraciously at Joanna's quim, until it seemed to have spread and enveloped him like a rubber mask and he was biting at the walls of her vagina and thrusting his tongue far up towards her soft cervix.

She grew more and more wild and whirling above him, squashing his face so that he could hardly breathe, falling away from him at times in her passion. Her breathing became a soft whistling whine of breath which rose to a level he could hardly hear. And then she sprang away from him with a rigid convulsion of her body and then squashed back, letting out a groaning exclamation as a flood of liquid seemed to cover his face, and he finished her off with a last swiping flourish of his tongue.

She slithered off him and fell in a limp heap on the floor. Catherine continued to slide up and down, tightly and sweetly and wonderfully on his prick, and now Emily leapt in to take her mother's place.

As he sucked her and she started to give fluttering little shouts, Adam felt his pulsating rod swelling up. Catherine was crying out to him: "Come, come, come!"

He tensed his limbs, pushing his hips up at her as she descended along his hard, fleshy length. He could feel the movement in his bowels, such sweet, unbearable movement. "Now, now!" Catherine yelled, her firm, young body shaking like a leaf as her own orgasm reached the point where it was about to flow over. Adam thrust up, gasping into the quim over his mouth. He felt his swollen prick tremble, hesitate, heard Catherine's shout of "Aaaaaaah!" and then he bit hard into Emily's nether lips and held on like a bulldog while he shot his load of sperm up into the sweet, youthful belly of his host's daughter.

He went on sucking as Catherine rolled off him, until he heard Emily crying out for him to stop but not wanting him to. He clutched her taut, impudent breasts and squeezed, and then he squeezed her soft, young buttocks, crushing them viciously like soft flowers he wanted to destroy. He poked a finger up her rectum and jiggled it around inside the soft, rubbery depths. Suddenly she screamed and jerked away; she rolled off the divan onto the floor beside her mother. She lay there using her legs as if she was cycling for a couple of seconds and then she shot them out straight and rigid and jack-knifed her body three times before she fell back in a state of abandon, her thighs wide apart, her eyes closed.

Adam relaxed and then he felt himself being pushed over onto his side, and where various fingers had already made the opening larger, he felt Dalmain's prick prodding in. He thought of resistance.

Dalmain whispered: "Just an interlude while you and they regain your breath ready for the next bout."

What the hell, Adam thought. It's all for the good of Art. And he pulled his legs up to make it easier and grunted with pain and excitement as Dalmain's prick went right up his bottom and began to bugger him for all it was worth.

CHAPTER SEVENTEEN

"...How tender 'tis to love the babe that milks me— I would, while it was smiling in my face, have plucked my nipple from his boneless gums, and dash'd the brains out had I so sworn as you have done to do this."

Eve was no longer Eve. She was Lady Macbeth. To herself she was Lady Macbeth and her performance was achieving some effect on the Duncans, though that might have been because it was late and everyone had drunk a lot.

Sir George Duncan said: "If we should fail?" And in the line as he said it there was all of Macbeth's anguish.

"We fail! But screw your courage to the sticking place and we'll fail not. When Duncan is asleep..."

This had been the suggestion of the Duncans, partly because Lady Celia had wanted to reduce Eve to a nonentity. But her performance was surprising them, having the very reverse effect. They let her go on, the two of them, while the rest of the party sat around in appreciative silence.

"All right," Sir George said, at last. "That'll do. You've made your point. You want to get on in the theatre and if talent has anything to do with it you should, my dear."

Eve smiled and somebody turned on the record-player and they all got up and began to dance. Lady Celia stared at Eve with eyes that still contained an ultimate hostility although it appeared she was trying to be friendly. She was rather drunk and her eyes burned more than ever and bored right through Eve's skull to her brain. Sir George went off to find another bottle, leaving them alone. Eve, too, was rather drunk, otherwise she would have been more reticent to read Lady Macbeth in front of such great theatre stars. In her present state and, with increasing familiarity, she no longer felt the awe of them she had at the first meeting. Everybody seemed to be the same underneath. They all wanted something from other people and if you could give it you got on with them, if you couldn't they ignored you.

She wasn't sure what her position was. She remembered something Harrod had said about them being a strange couple. She looked around the room to take her thoughts off insoluble mysteries. It was a banqueting hall. The place was a veritable mansion in its own ground to the southwest of London. The courtyard when she'd arrived on foot, having come from the station, was crammed with cars and champagne, and Scotch had been flowing inside. It seemed that these people lived on champagne and Scotch and canapes. And here, as always, they had the run of the house. People disappeared onto the terraces, into the upper rooms, into the grounds. There seemed to be a tacit understanding that anything went. The Duncan mansion was exactly the way she had always imagined a baronial castle. Wide stairway from the entrance hall leading to landing which led off at both sides to a series of rooms. The banqueting hall opened off the entrance hall to one side of the stairs and the kitchens were somewhere through other rooms at the other side. Everywhere there was oak panelling and parquet flooring with rich red carpets and hangings at strategic points and chandeliers descending in glinting cascades of glass from the ceilings. The champagne was drunk from silver goblets as a change from the usual glasses and the canapes were piled on silver salvers. There were other dishes, too, of salads with various meats and fishes. And there were cigarettes everywhere in little wooden pots.

It had been eight o'clock when Eve arrived. It was now two in the morning and, as far as she could tell, nobody at all of the forty or so guests had left—or even looked like leaving. Sir George had invited her to stay the night, adding that he would show her to her room later.

Eve came out of her reverie to find Lady Celia moving over towards her.

"Would you like to come upstairs?" she asked. "There's something I'd like to show you."

There was something in Lady Celia's manner that Eve didn't trust, some underlying urgency which belied the casual nature of her words...

"What is it?" Eve asked.

"Wait and see," Lady Celia said. "I don't suppose you've seen one before."

Eve followed her from the banqueting hall. There was something about those burning eyes that both fascinated and repelled her; the strength of the woman's personality was overwhelming.

They went out and up the broad stairs and along the interior balcony to a door at the end. Lady Celia unlocked the door, let them in and then locked it behind them. Eve watched her, half tipsily, feeling that she had walked into a trap and should make some protest, but quite unable to do so.

The room was a rose-coloured bedroom—a boudoir. It was too full of Lady Celia's things for it possibly to have anything to do with Sir George. There was a smell of incense rather than perfume and the room was in some indefinable way rather unfeminine. It was dominated by a huge fourposter bed of the really old-fashioned kind, with a curtain you could close all the way round it. There were the usual wardrobes and dressing tables and big French windows opening out onto a balcony. There were also a surprising number of mirrors all around the room, including a couple of loose ones leaning against the wall in a corner.

Lady Celia went to the windows and drew heavy, red curtains across. She turned back to Eve and studied her, every inch of her.

"You're a very lovely girl," she said.

Eve stared at her, embarrassed, not knowing what to say.

"I can help you get into a West End production," she said. "If you're willing to do something for me, that is."

"A West End production?"

"A West End production. It goes without saying that I have a great deal of influence—and you have beauty and talent. That is a formidable combination for success on the stage."

"It would be wonderful if you could help me," Eve said. She was torn between a stomach-chilling delight and a nervous apprehension caused solely by the avidity of those eyes devouring her.

Lady Celia came close to her, the blazing eyes penetrating deep at a foot's range. Eve felt quite unnerved and had to fight down a creeping desire to run to the door and batter on it for help.

The woman's hand reached out and touched Eve's cheek, while the eyes held her as if she were under hypnosis. She stood stockstill while the fingers ran down to her lips and moved gently along them and then over her chin to the long, smooth neck. She shivered.

"A very lovely girl," Lady Celia said, as if to herself. "Do you go to bed with many men?" she asked.

Eve was almost afraid to answer.

"Not *many,*" she said finally.

"You're much too good for them," Lady Celia said. "Men don't appreciate anything."

Eve stayed rooted to the spot as the eyes came nearer and the fingers dropped to her breast. She felt as if she were being strangled, but quite unable to resist. Was this the way rabbits felt as the weasel approached? She caught the smell of champagne from Lady Celia's breath and felt the pressure of her dress very slightly against her own. She found she couldn't move as the face came close to hers, as if this was what she wanted. The lips, Lady Celia's lips, closed down on hers, gently at first, so that she could feel the full, sharply delinated imprint, and then more furiously. Eve felt her own lips, rigid at first, slowly relax under the pressure and then, as the tongue clove into her mouth, she gave way completely and let the body follow it up, rubbing hard against her, with loins undulating.

"My lovely girl," Lady Celia breathed. "I will help you, if you will help me."

Eve didn't answer, simply put her own tongue out against the tongue that invaded her mouth.

Lady Celia's hands caressed her breasts with a woman's knowledge, and ran down her sides and her back, while their bodies locked together. After a bit she broke away, gasping, her eyes still dominating, leaping almost from her head. She moved away to a wardrobe, opened it, rummaged behind a pile of clothes folded in a heap on its floor and produced a strange instrument, strange, but immediately recognisable. Eve looked at it in fascination. She had a very queer feeling in the pit of her stomach. The intimate touch of another woman on her had excited and revolted her in almost equal proportions, the combined effect of the two emotions leaving her bereft of any power to act.

The instrument was a solid rubber length in the shape of a male organ. Attached to it were two empty rubber testicles and the base of the imitation penis had a leather strap long enough to stretch round a pair of hips attached to it. Another strap ran from the testicles to fit between a pair of thighs and join the first strap at the back where they were buckled together.

Lady Celia brought the object out and fondled it, looking at Eve with a deep, sexy expression.

"I want to do this to you and then have you do it to me," she said.

Eve simply stared at the instrument and Lady Celia came over to her and led her towards the bed.

"Let's take off our clothes," she said.

Eve felt dazed, not really knowing what to do. Her upbringing had never accepted this sort of thing. But Lady Celia had promised to help her and also... like the man who takes his first shot of heroin, she found something horridly fascinating about it.

Lady Celia began to strip with hands that shook. She was naked in two minutes flat, standing watching Eve, her slim, firm, slightly muscular body quivering with anticipation.

Eve fumbled with a zip fastener. Her fingers trembled. Lady Celia, her naked body exuding a warmth which Eve could feel before she reached her, came over and began to undress her with gentle, expert fingers.

Eve closed her eyes. She began to tremble all over at the strange forbiddenness of the situation. The alien fingers crept over her like spiders, undoing intimate buttons, brushing against normally hidden areas of flesh, slowly, relentlessly peeling her covering to the point where all resistance would be quite hopeless.

"My beauty, my beauty," Lady Celia whispered.

She stood back and looked over Eve's nude body. Her cheeks burned with a furious lustre and her eyes were now like black gems. Eve stood like a statue, the air cool on her nakedness, the points of her breasts hard, a painful constriction in her chest and loins.

Lady Celia came close to her, rubbed her own naked body against Eve's so that the nipples of their breasts met and the breasts of the one crushed those of the other. Lady Celia's thighs twined around Eve's and her muff of pubic hair brushed warmly against that of Eve's. She felt Eve's buttocks and pulled them apart to caress the tight anus with her finger and then she dropped on her knees and began to shower kisses on the thighs and then on the triangle of raised flesh between them and then, inching the legs apart, on the soft, moistening flesh between the thighs. A huge shudder ran down Eve's spine and petered out somewhere amongst her toes as Lady Celia's unyielding lips closed on her clitoris. She felt quite out of her depth, and yet the sexual stimulation was enormous, with that additional chill that a real sense of indulging in something sinful always gives.

Lady Celia pushed her back towards the bed and she fell over backwards onto it, sinking into it as if it were a haystack.

Lady Celia followed, pulling Eve's thighs up against her shoulders, burying her face in Eve's quim, licking and sucking like a maniac.

Eve was quite inarticulate with still conflicting emotions when Lady Celia suddenly left her. Eve opened her eyes and saw her hostess take the instrument and disappear into an adjoining room. She heard a tap running and then Lady Celia reappeared. She was wearing the false genitals, the cock standing out long and stiff from her triangle of hair, the balls hanging down between her thighs. But now the balls, too, were bloated.

"Hot water," Lady Celia said. "Half a gallon to empty into your pretty little cunt. No man could ever do that for you."

Eve lay still, with her thighs apart, her heart beating so loudly she felt something would burst inside her, her belly heaving as if she were already being screwed to the very core.

Lady Celia flowed down onto the bed, her body half covering Eve's, her ruthless hands explored again and her lips plucked at the nipples at the breasts, at any part of the expanse of flesh which was offered her.

"My lovely, lovely darling," Lady Celia whispered and her eyes were hard and ruthless in her passion. "I'm going to screw you as no man ever has or could. I want to see you squirm and cry out in helpless passion."

The tension in Eve's body was unbearable. Still something inside her had refused to relax.

"Open your legs wide, sweetheart, I'm coming in now," Lady Celia whispered.

Mechanically, quivering like a frightened horse, Eve opened her thighs wider. Lady Celia's body came over onto hers. She felt the woman arranging her hips between the obtuse angle formed by the two thighs. She closed her eyes, held her breath and waited, knowing that this was the point of final surrender.

The rubber prick slid into her cunt and went up and up and up without quarter, drawing a long expulsion of breath from Eve's tormented lungs.

"O dear god, dear god," she cried and, for some reason, tears came into her eyes.

Lady Celia sank into her, breathing fiercely. She began to work her hips like an Amazon. Her hands oozed all over Eve like a dozen snakes, searching and entering and pulling apart and digging to allow her no part of herself that was still her own. The cock was enormously long and thick. When Lady Celia thrust in the last half inch, Eve jerked in pain. But there was no escape now, and she didn't want it anyway. Lady Celia held her in a vice-like grip, pressing down on her with all the weight of her slim, muscular body, gripping now her shoulders, now her waist, now her buttocks with fingers like whipcord.

It was like being impaled on a stake. Thrust after thrust shot up into Eve's helpless loins to explode in a spark of pain at each apex. Eve began to thresh about. Her body had gone now into the relaxed realms of complete acceptance. Her loins were a mass of consuming flame and her breasts were painful as if they, too, wanted to burst and be free.

"You beauty, beauty!" Lady Celia kept muttering. And every time she said it she gritted her teeth and gave an extra twist to the in-thrust or swooped down and bit Eve's lips until blood flowed from them.

"You're mine, mine, mine," Lady Celia murmured and her fingers gripped Eve's shoulders until they bruised, or her buttocks until she squealed for them to be released. And all the time she made rushing sallies into Eve's cunt with the prick which stood up straight and never-yielding as a ramrod, tearing straight up to the cervix and tickling it apart with every stroke.

Eve began to respond wildly to the screwing. She'd never been fucked like this before. The organ was so huge. It was like handing over one's soul. She would have done anything, promised anything for the rhythmic penetration to continue. Had it stopped she felt she would have died. In fact, that became her great fear: that Lady Celia might tire.

"Don't stop," she breathed. "Don't ever stop or I shall die." And her own hands dug into the feminine shoulders which wriggled against her, and moved down the splendid, firm, sinewy back of the leading lady of the English stage who had turned out to be the leading Liz as well.

Eve's climax was fast coming. The determined rhythm, the consistent stroke and the hugeness of the tool brought her quickly up to fever pitch.

"Come my darling creature, come!" Lady Celia urged and she quickened up the rhythm like a rowing crew raising the rate of the stroke.

"Oh, it's beautiful, beautiful," Eve shrieked. Between her thighs was one mass of sweet, wet sensitivity which grew more and more sharp in its sensitivity with every second, reaching up to a pinpoint of needle-sharp feeling, until suddenly from this pinpoint would explode and tumble an incredible weight of aching feeling.

Lady Celia's eyes filled her vision. They were slit in a ruthless joy of possession and of power.

"There and there and there," she grunted as she rammed the artificial cock deep into Eve's belly.

"I can't stand it," Eve screamed. "It's too much... too much..." Her voice died in a strangled mixture of sob and sigh and then broke out again in a high-pitched scream as her passion overflowed all bounds and swept through her loins like a jet fighter racing towards the sun and suddenly exploding in a puff of smoke against the great molten disc.

And as she came, Lady Celia squeezed the mock balls between her thighs and the hot fluid rushed through a narrow tube in the centre of the penis and spurted into Eve's vagina like a tidal wave...

A little later, Lady Cella strapped the contraption onto Eve's loins, arranged one of the spare mirrors at the head of the bed, turned sideways to it, knelt on all fours and had Eve screw her from behind for three-quarters of an hour, while—as long as she could keep her head still—she watched Eve's movement in the glass.

It was only after the last ounce of energy had been drawn out of them and they lay exhausted, their bodies lightly touching, that a piece of the ceiling opened like a trapdoor and Sir George peered through.

"Wonderful," he said. "I've lived through every second of it."

CHAPTER EIGHTEEN

The gallery was crowded with a colourful array of people. It was a large one in Bond Street—an extra large one on two floors. Dalmain had done him so proud, Adam thought, he'd had difficulty finding enough paintings to fill the exhibition space. Now they were all tastefully arranged on a white background with plenty of space for each so that the viewers could really concentrate on each separately.

Dalmain, himself, had marked up the prices—and what prices he'd decided to mark up! Adam had been horrified and then flattered and then he'd come to realise how necessary it was to price so high if you wanted to impress the majority of the people who might buy.

Dalmain had told him: "You must realise the power of publicity—and that includes self-publicity. It's one of the wonders of the modern world that you only have to paint a picture and then go and stand on your head for an hour with it outside Piccadilly underground station and people will gather, you'll be written up in the popular press, interviewed—perhaps satirically, but it doesn't matter—by at least one of the quality papers and you'll sell your painting and create the market for more so that someone has to give you an exhibition. This principle, in various ways and to varying degrees applies to almost anything: witness the beatniks, the angry young men, etcetera. That they may have talent is beside the point. Many people have talent tenfold but only get across to a small audience because they don't stand on their heads, so to speak.

"Now, about the prices of your paintings. If they're put on in my gallery *and* outrageous prices are charged, that in itself is publicity. You'll see, my dear Adam, that tomorrow some newspaper is going to draw attention to the ridiculous prices being charged for an unknown painter. Another will follow by agreeing and expressing surprise that these prices are charged for paintings exhibited in my gallery and viewed by this very select bunch of viewers. What is the idea, they will ask? And the fact that they are asking will create a mystery, a public one, which will interest more and more people until nobody can afford not to know anything about your paintings. It is a very simple matter, dear boy. All you need is a sense of humour in the very real sense. Remember that this whole aspect has nothing to do with art as far as you are concerned; it has to do with what people are prepared to pay for the notorious, the hugely publicised. You will see."

Adam listened to all this in fascination. And he watched the viewers in fascination. They were, of course, all people who could afford these inflated prices if they so chose. His paintings impressed. They were good, after all. Many people were introduced to him, but the selling ball started rolling after he'd met the nymphomaniac wife of a shipowner, an elegant cosmopolitan woman of uncertain nationality.

She held his hand rather long, said she thought he had enormous talent, but she wasn't sure whether to buy because she liked to know the sort of ideas an artist had before she decided whether or not to support him. Adam was confused by this, but encouraged by a big wink from Dalmain.

Would he care, she asked, to have dinner with her on her husband's yacht off the Isle of Wight next week-end—say Friday. Her husband would unfortunately not be there, but that would mean they could get to know each other even better. Her gorgeous, longing eyes looked right through his mind to his genitals and Adam said he would be delighted, and they made the date.

"Good," the shipowner's wife said. "Well, to show that I think your talent is very considerable, quite apart from your views, I think I'll take the five red and blue compositions with the seagulls and guitars along the end of the upper gallery."

She took a chequebook from the little crocodile skin handbag and wrote out a cheque. Adam could hardly control his breathing. It was fabulous—he was on the way to being a rich man. Several people watched this rapid transaction and the word flew round the galleries. Mrs. Goldenbaum appeared from nowhere and showed some solicitousness about Adam, wondering what exactly had taken place betwen him and the other woman. Then, not to be outdone, she ordered another five. And the ball really started rolling. Within an hour, every painting in the gallery had been sold and Dalmain was on the telephone to a number of newspapers to tell them the news.

Within another hour, Adam had been interviewed by a number of reporters—different people with different functions from the art critics.

By the time everyone had left, including Mrs. Golden-baum, whom Adam was to meet later at the Dorchester,

Dalmain was smiling with amused triumph at how completely his words had been borne out and he and Adam toasted themselves in a special old brandy for a change.

Adam felt enormously grateful to Dalmain.

"When I see her at the weekend," he said, "I'll make her into a witch. Then you'll be able to have a go to."

CHAPTER NINETEEN

Eve studied the newspapers with increasing admiration. She was spending another weekend with Sir George and Lady Celia. Lady Celia had a bad cold coming on, which might turn out to be influenza. Even her lovemaking had been rather laboured due to her difficulty in breathing, but she'd performed with her usual gusto and Eve was rather sore in her rectum.

She sat on her bottom now in a garden chair, tensing her buttocks to ease the discomfort and learning all about Adam's success. After seeing the Daily Dandy, she'd ordered all the others available at the village shop. It was remarkable. As she read the reports it was difficult to realise that Adam had become a national figure overnight. His total sale had reaped an amazing financial return and the critics, whilst hardly reacting in the bowled-over manner of the buyers, were treating his work with considerable respect, particularly in view of his youth. There were paragraphs about him in all the gossip columns, mentions of him at fashionable parties, one or two searching interviews about his likes and dislikes, humble origins, single-mindedness. Eve could hardly take it all in. In spite of the way he'd treated her during their last meeting on the Common, she felt she wanted to telephone him and offer her congratulations. But one thing stopped her from doing this—her own lack of success. She felt it would seem that she was wanting to make up to him purely because of his triumph, and in spite of her machinations on her own behalf, she did not consider Adam a fit subject to kow-tow to.

She saw his handsome face, full and profile, in a dozen newspapers. He had got there first, but she would follow. She put down the papers on the wicker table and leaned back in the cool spring air. She would follow all right. She reflected on the past few weeks. Everyone was eating out of her hand. Rushton gave her the best roles and nonetheless allowed her to stand down from them any evening she liked as long as she gave him a couple of days' notice. He'd accepted that she now had her own contacts in London and that she was furthering her career. He had no choice if he still wanted to exercise his longing prick on her occasionally—and that he did.

Lady Celia, in the meantime, could hardly see enough of her. She was extremely possessive and sometimes so savage in lovemaking that Eve was half frightened that she might suddenly produce a knife and use it instead of the makebelieve penis. Sir George had continued to watch them through the one-way glass in the ceiling; it had been an open secret. It appeared that in the normal act he was impotent, but that he could achieve an orgasm jacking off while he watched two women screwing in that way—particularly if they were women with whom he had intimate relations in the spiritual sense.

His impotency had fascinated Eve—and presented her with a challenge. She'd got into the habit of wandering around their house dressed only in a bathrobe and this she had sometimes left open in Sir George's presence, sometimes slipped off completely when alone in a room and knowing he was likely to come in. The net result was that one evening when Lady Celia gone to pay a short visit to friends in the nearby town, he'd come across Eve displaying her pretty little ass provocatively and decided to try to overcome his affliction. He'd grabbed her and fucked her hard, bending her over the back of an easy chair. He'd worked himself up, but failed to pass that seemingly impenetrable barrier. He'd come so near, however, that it had given him hope. From then on he'd watched and waited for opportunities until, finally, with Lady Celia's absence again in the nearby town, he'd pinned Eve down on the very bed where she and his wife had earlier rampaged. He'd arranged the mirrors all around, had her suck him for half an hour and then shoved his penis first in her quim for another half hour and then in her ass for a final effort.

Eve had been so sore and aching in her vagina and her back passage that she'd been on the point, having come several times herself during his efforts, of asking him to give over, when his breath had started mounting again in a furious spiral of sound. She'd revived her flagging interest and screwed her bum hard and cooperatively back onto his fat skewer. She'd heard his breathing grow to the volume of a baby hurricane, heard him cry: "No, it's not possible, not possible!"

She'd thundered her soft behind back at his loins, then, shouting: "Yes it is, it is—you can!"

So they had seemed to battle for several minutes. Her energy and determination against his disbelief and built-in anticipation of failure. Until, all at once, he'd begun to choke as if he were really going to be sick and then he'd come so hard that she'd felt the solid heat of it fill her like a lake flooding through a dam to the dried up valley below.

Afterwards they'd lain for a long time on the bed together while he marveled at what had happened and talked to her about his long history of failure. They had decided that no hint of what had happened should by given to Lady Celia. Although she didn't mind her husband watching her own indulgence, his dallying with her girl would hardly be tolerated.

From then on the psychological barrier was smashed. Sir George was able to come every time he screwed Eve and he had come to depend upon her for his sexual-emotional neeeds to the exclusion of all else.

So while Lady Celia was working to get Eve a meaty part in a new West End production, due on in some months' time, Sir George, under Eve's direction, began to work in a completely different channel. He began to encourage his wife in all sort of subtle ways to get influenza: walking on wet grass after an all-night blind, going out into chilly air from great heat without adequate clothing. The slightest hints and suggestions—a mere indication that he thought she was being unnecessarily fussy in wanting to put on a shawl, or to dry her hair after washing it before they went for a drive.

The plan had worked. Lady Celia was in the foothills of influenza now. If it worsened, she would be unable to continue with her role in *A View from the Bridge,* which was having a long run. In that case an understudy would have to be brought in. Sir George had already seen to that. He was making it worth the understudy's while financially, plus the promise of a good part in a forthcoming production, to have her old mother in the Shetlands fall ill just about the time of his wife's affliction. He was then going to bring all pressure to bear to get Eve, who had been rehearsing the role for some time under his secret tutoring, into the part.

What was the harm? Eve had asked during his

initial doubts. Lady Celia would recover after a week or a fortnight. By then Eve would have made or failed to make a bigger impact by reason of the inevitable comparison with Lady Celia than she'd ever have made in a new play, and the normal understudy would have lost nothing tangible and gained a great deal materially.

"It's the best present you could possibly give me," she'd told Sir George, who so frequently expressed his desire to buy her a castle in thanks for the new pleasures she'd opened up for him.

Lady Celia came out into the grounds now and wandered over to Eve. It was Eve, now, who felt the more powerful; more powerful than both of them put together.

"Darling, I really feel quite sick," Lady Celia said, without bothering to sit down. "In fact, I must go to bed with some hot rum and milk and a hot water bottle. You will stay until tomorrow so that I can see you, won't you? Perhaps I'll feel better then."

Eve knew what that suggestion meant. At the moment, Lady Celia felt *hors de combat.*

"Yes dear," she said. "Of course I will. You go to bed and I'll make your rum and hot milk myself. Then I'll have a game of snap with George until bedtime."

"Sweetie," Lady Celia said. She leaned down to kiss Eve, but thought better of it and straightened.

"I don't want you to get my cold," she explained.

CHAPTER TWENTY

There was a moment's electric silence behind the curtain as it swung down in its peculiar progression of little jerks to cut the audience off from the stage.

Eve glanced nervously at Sir George—Eddie Carbone, rather—and he smiled at her and raised a thumb. And then the applause broke out and the curtain began to go up again.

The cast moved forward into a line across the stage and the applause came at them in great waves of sound and seemed to lift them off their feet. It was tremendous. The actors' and actresses' eyes were alight with recognition. There seemed to have been a new spirit in the play tonight after the way it had settled into a standard of high consistency over the past months. They had felt it—and they had felt the response coming from the audience, that sense of the audience being right with them on their side—not only with the applause at the intervals, but during the whole production.

Various members of the cast stepped forward for their own separate ovations. And then Sir George stepped forward and the ovation lifted to a crescendo. And then he, with a gallant gesture—contrived long before the evening—stretched back his hand to the courageous understudy who had stepped into that impossible breach.

Eve moved forward and the crescendo became a crescendo of crescendos, if such a thing were possible. Shouts of "Bravo" rang out through the building. The clapping became that strange, humming ovation which includes feet and the human voice as well as the hands.

Sir George stepped back suddenly, leaving Eve in the centre of the stage in front of the smiling cast. The action was an effective one, accentuating still more the role she had played and his view of the honour she deserved. An opinion thus given could not be ignored and the applause went on and on with the curtain going up and down until there seemed a hint almost of hopefulness in the way it flopped to the boards. The lights went up but still the applause continued and it was only the first bars of the national anthem which quelled the fervour to a reluctant but respectful silence.

The cast gathered around Eve as the anthem died and the audience began to file out of the theatre with much chattering and scraping of feet.

"You were wonderful, Eve," Sir George said quietly in a voice suitably restrained for the public nature of the occasion.

"And so say all of us," piped up the various voices.

"A party," Sir George cried. "A party to celebrate—a late supper with champagne!"

There were cheers all around and they hurried off to remove their makeup.

Eve stood on the empty stage with Sir George. There was a little fire of satisfaction inside her and an indefinable sadness that now the hurdle was past. She looked up at her companion.

"How do you think everyone'll like it?" she asked, "honestly?"

"They'll rave," he told her. "Don't give it another thought. My reputation is staked on it."

CHAPTER TWENTY-ONE

Adam lounged on a foam mattress on the deck of the handsome yacht with the newspapers spread in front of him in untidy profusion.

Celeste Manzoni, the shipowner's wife, came up from the companion hatch wearing a white bikini which covered very little of her elegant proportions. She was a superb bronze. Her skin shone like a polished shield. She looked for Adam through her dark glasses, saw him and came strolling over. Even when she walked her hips seemed to quiver with sexual desire.

Adam looked up and watched her approach. He just hoped her husband stayed away a little longer. The night of tossing and heaving on the narrow bunk in her berth, with the silent, silky sea showing through the porthole, had been unutterable bliss. Her body had been warm as the sun, her clinging quim as cool and caressing as the tepid water of the sea. She had been insatiable. If it hadn't been for the lazy day they'd spent yesterday, he would not have felt so fresh today.

She settled down beside him. The small crew had been sent ashore for the weekend and they were alone. She ran her long, slim hand down his back and smiled.

"How does it feel to be suddenly so famous and the lover of one of the richest women in the world—" she asked.

"The latter makes the former seem superfluous," Adam said.

She smiled, happily, at his flattery and ran her hand over his chest.

"For that," she said, "I'll only allow you an hour's rest instead of two."

Adam laughed and kissed her hand.

She glanced at the newspapers.

"Who is this girl they're making such a fuss of?" she asked.

"A new stage star," Adam said, casually. "Taken the world by storm."

"How wonderful to have real artistic talent," Celeste Manzoni said, "instead of being just a spectator on the sidelines like me."

"Nonsense," Adam said. "You have superb talent in the greatest art in the world."

She broke into a peal of laughter and pulled him over so that his head was cushioned between her breasts. She removed the brassiere so that his face lay against her bare breasts.

"Let me know if you see a helicopter," she said.

Adam closed his eyes, letting the sun seep into them, hot and relaxing through the eyelids. She reached round him and picked up one of the newspapers.

"Good heavens," she said. "They say she's better in the role than Lady Celia Duncan!"

"I know," Adam said. "Unbelievable isn't it?"

His mind went back to the few short months ago when he and Eve has sat in the gods looking down from a height on the play in which she was now proving so successful. A height and a distance seemingly unbridgeable. And now... what a way they had come.

"I wonder who she is," Celeste mused. "I've never heard of her before and I thought I knew everybody, those arriving as well as those arrived."

"She was in some provincial rep," Adam said. "Got to know the right people, I expect."

She looked down at him curiously.

"You sound rather cynical for one so young," she said.

"Do you think it's not true. How else would she suddenly get such a part?"

"You must be right," she agreed. "How fascinating. I think I must invite her to a party."

Adam fell silent. He hadn't seen Eve for a long time. Her image recurred in his brain every so often and when, as today, he heard mention of her, he felt a pang of nostalgia and guilt. The guilt was for the beating he'd given her. In the calm following the act, he'd begun to feel that it was really not his business to commit violence on her just because she'd allowed one or two men to have her in what he now saw was the furtherance of her career. After all, he'd done just that himself, hadn't he? What irked him always was the fact that she had consistently refused him so that eventually the only way he'd been able to make love to her was to take her by force.

"Penny for them?"

He looked along at Celeste's rounded brown limbs which stretched out at right angles to his own prostrate body. He tried to recall the details of Eve's body, but could only remember the vague salient features.

"I was wondering who else you'd have, if you had a party," he said. "I'd feel jealous if you had too many Counts and Cabinet Ministers trying to make you."

"They wouldn't stand a chance," she said, looking glowingly down at him. "Not the Prime Minister nor the Duke of Edinburgh, nor the Shah of Persia. They're old men—and they're not artists."

"Shall I paint your portrait?" Adam asked, stroking her leg.

"You might make me ugly."

"No, I would paint you with me making love to you. You would be doubly beautiful then."

"How would we pose."

"Like this," Adam said.

He twisted round and pushed her back on the mattress, coming down on top of her.

His hands caressed her bare breasts.

"But how will you paint it?" she gasped.

"From memory."

She pressed her body hard against his.

"Hurry, darling," she pleaded. "Screw me quickly. My portrait will be the most passionate that's ever been painted."

A few minutes later as he threaded into her loins like a needle running through soft cloth, Adam felt that with every thrust which brought a grimace of feeling from her he was moulding her picture like a sculptor his clay.

CHAPTER TWENTY-TWO

Far out on the horizon dark and white specks passed with smudges of smoke above them blemishing the light blue of the sky. The sea was flecked white and in the distance appeared to be glazed and calm, though closer to the boat there were small waves. It was a wonderful balmy day which might almost have been transported from the Mediterranean had it not been for the slight freshness in the air and the comparatively muted colours.

A rowing boat scudded out from the shore where, far off, thousands of people were lying on the beaches getting sun-tanned, dropping sandwich papers, playing with children, buying ice creams, riding donkeys...

"Here comes another lot," Celeste said, leaning over the boat-rail beside Adam. "I wonder if our famous actress will be aboard?"

"I wonder?" Adam was preoccupied.

The deck was already littered with people arrived for the party. The lounge below was also full of them and the chink of ice tinkled above the conversation.

"She agreed to."

Would she come, Adam wondered, if she knew he were there? Would she know he might be? Probably. The gossip hounds would provide her with plenty of sources. He thought bitterly, yet again, of those insinuating columns in which names were linked, as if innocently, but with all the suggestion in the world. His name had been linked with that of Celeste by a variety of verbal formulae used in these interfering gutter columns: "Exceptionally frequent visitor of late aboard the..." "Seen often these past weeks in the company of..." And so on. The penalty of being famous; what you ate became famous too, and how many times you said good morning between breakfast and lunch, and whom you had a cup of coffee with, and naturally whom you were sleeping with. The implications had been so clear that Grace Goldenbaum had written to Adam from Paris asking him what he thought he was up to and Celeste's husband had cabled from a business conference in New York. Things had been smoothed over, of course. One defence to that sort of intrusion is that many of the famous come to learn that the suggestions amount to absolutely nothing except unutterable tastelessness and inhumanity on the part of those who make them. Except that, naturally, sometimes the insinuations are one hundred per cent correct. The best thing, as always, was to carry on as before, never allowing the limelight to force you into separation or hiding, with its implication of guilt, and this is what Celeste and Adam had done, thus continuing an affair of great sexual satisfaction to both of them.

"That looks like her pictures—the girl sitting in the stern."

Celeste sounded quite excited, and Adam, knowing exactly who and what Eve was felt a surge of astonishment that this social queen could be in the slightest moved by somebody so ordinary.

But then was Eve ordinary? In the sense that attracted Celeste, he realised, she wasn't. Apart from her talent

—and here was someone who could actually do something—the very fact that she'd gained the position she had indicated certain qualities of character which, obviously, could be fascinating to strangers. She was like him. They both had an elemental quality of toughness that these rich socialites lacked.

Yes, it was Eve all right: that champagne hair blown out in the breeze, that firm elegance with that suggestion of the oriental, so elusive one wasn't really sure it was there at all. She was wearing dark glasses and looking towards the boat. It seemed to Adam she was staring straight at him.

"I'm going down to get a drink," he said.

"Don't you want to meet our new star?"

"Later."

He went down the steps of the companion way, smiled at a beautiful girl sitting on the floor, who stretched out her long brown legs in silent invitation and smiled sleepily back.

He poured himself a large Scotch and soda and walked back to the companion way. He climbed up the steps and sat on one near the top. He heard the scraping noises of the rowing boat alongside and listened hard but could hear nothing beyond the anonymous hum of conversation which enveloped the yacht like an aura.

But then he heard Celeste's voice leading the way along towards the companion way.

"...yes, you need gallons... and I suppose you have to look after your voice very carefully, anyway."

And then Eve's voice.

"I never think about that. I just like champagne, really chilled, and with a hot day to go with it."

They came nearer and, although he wanted to move away so that he wouldn't be bothered, he found himself continuing to sit on the steps waiting for them to virtually fall over him.

"Here we are," Celeste said, appearing against the rectangle of sky above. "I'll lead the way."

She saw Adam.

"Oh there you are, Adam. I'd like you to meet Eve Patten."

She turned back, making the introductions.

Eve stopped a couple of steps above Adam and looked at him with the blank discs of glass.

"How do you do," she said.

"How do you do," Adam replied.

Eve looked lovely to him. He recalled her features with a sense of physical shock now that she stood before him. She was a little more carefully made up than she used to be, a little more elegantly dressed and there was an even greater air of confidence about her bearing. The contrast between her air of calm self-possession, awareness of her own beauty at this moment and the sweating, flailing, sobbing figure he'd raped some months ago was strangely moving to both heart and loins.

"Did you say champagne?" he asked.

"We'll all have some," Celeste said.

Adam left them chatting and went through the lounge deck to the bar, exchanging a brief, pick-me-up smile with the girl on the floor. The barman poured the champagne and gave him a tray.

"So you've been one of these absolutely single-minded people," Celeste was saying, when he got back to them. "Adam is another. I do admire you so. It's the only way to achieve anything."

"We seem to have achieved success more or less at the same moment," Eve said, looking at Adam.

He couldn't tell what her thoughts might be behind the vizor of those dark glasses.

"I still have some way to go," Adam said.

"We both have, haven't we?"

"Well, here's to the end of the road, whatever it might be," Celeste said. She looked from one to the other curiously as if something in their demeanour was not quite normal.

A white-coated steward came down the steps and approached them.

"Telephone call for you, Madame," he said.

Celeste checked a grimace, which Adam was intended to see.

"That'll be my husband," she said. She looked at him. "Perhaps you'll look after Miss Patten while I'm away. Shan't be long."

She disappeared up the companion way, leaving the two of them together, silent and embarrassed.

"Is your champagne chill enough?" Adam asked after a moment.

Eve began to giggle, suddenly in tiny, half stifled bursts. Adam stared at her for a moment and then he too began to laugh.

"Have you forgiven me?" he asked, when they managed to calm down.

"Forgiven you? Of course," Eve said. "I deserved it after the way I treated you." She paused. "And anyway, it wasn't so bad," she added, smiling behind the glasses.

"I hated you," he said. "I could still get pangs thinking about all that I didn't know."

"You don't still hate me?"

"Too much to think about."

She laughed.

"She's very beautiful, isn't she," she said.

"Who—Celeste? Yes, I suppose she is."

"Are the stories true?"

"What stories?"

She chucked her tongue.

"Don't worry, Adam," she said, "I wouldn't tell a soul."

"Nor would I," he said.

She laughed.

"How's the painting?" she asked.

"Pretty good. I've got exhibitions in Paris, Rome and New York, one after the other, through to the winter and I'm already making thousands. But I'm not working as hard as I used to."

"Wine, women and painting don't go together?"

"How about you? How do you find wine, men and acting?"

"Well, I'm working as hard as ever. The discipline's imposed from outside, of course. I've had a lot of offers for the future, including an enormous one from J. Arthur Rank."

"We'll be millionaires before we're thirty," Adam said.

"Have you missed me?" Eve asked, ignoring his statement.

"As much as you've missed me," Adam said.

"You've missed me a lot, then?"

"All right."

"Can I have another glass of champagne?" she asked. "I feel more like it than I have for months."

CHAPTER TWENTY-THREE

The water was warm, but cooling to the body after the sun's heat. The boat had receded to a miniature reproduction of itself and the water seemed deep and alien so far out in the bay.

Adam and Eve swam in leisurely towards the outer sea, a few feet apart. Their brown arms and bodies glistened in the sparkling water and could be seen palely under the surface. They had left the boat in a state of embalmment, bronzed bodies stretched out in the sun all over the place, with every cabin and berth occupied. Celeste had had to go ashore to follow out some instruction of her husband. She had left reluctantly, wanting as she had to spend the afternoon in bed with Adam. However, the necessity for some sort of discretion had swayed her not to insist on his accompanying her.

So he and Eve—she in the briefest of bikinis which revealed more than they concealed—and he in a tiny pair of trunks which were more like a g-string—had taken the opportunity to drift away from the madding crowd.

"How beautiful it is," Eve said, floating over on her stomach and gazing back at the shore line.

"There are more beautiful places," Adam said.

"No, I mean the life—all those riches, the way you're outside the rest of the world."

"Allied with our creative urges, those riches could provide the ideal existence," Adam said. "But they're not that much good to her."

"What a pity that the right combinations never fit together."

"We'll get there," Adam said.

They had been swimming towards a buoy, huge and gaunt and rather rusty, bobbing gently on the slight swell. Eve reached it and caught hold of one of the several handgrips.

Adam swam up beside her and his hand touched her shoulder as he too reached out for a grip. She turned and looked at him, her finely-chiseled features catching a golden glint from the sun.

"I wish," she said, "that our first time hadn't been in such awful, angry circumstances."

He leaned over and kissed her and they slammed together under the water, splashing gently as their bodies moved in contact. Her tongue came out and into his mouth, smooth as a little sea fish.

"It was your fault that they weren't," he said.

"I know... I know."

Her hand ran down and over his almost naked buttocks and then crossed his hip lightly to caress the large bulk of his genitals under the tiny triangle of silk.

"There were things I had to do to get where I am," she said.

The gentle touch of her hand, like a probing octupus, filled him with all the old longings for her that had never been consumated except in violence and anger. He didn't care about the past. He wanted her body.

"I know," he said. "We're the same, as I said."

He ran his free hand down her back. It was strong and supple with a hint of gooseflesh from the coolness of the water. He stroked her buttocks, wet and silky and rounded tight under the little bikini. He brought his hand up around her body and stroked the taut volume of her left breast, simultaneously feeling the large part which was naked, the smaller part which was covered by the flimsy brassiere. He kissed her again and saw the deep desire that made her limbs fight against the water towards him. She had his prick up hard now and was squeezing it between her thumb and the tips of her fingers.

"Can we do it here?" she asked, looking out over the water.

Adam surveyed the horizon: the boat in the far distance, others beyond it nearer to the crowded shore. It was so far away; they could have been in the middle of an ocean. True someone might race out in a speedboat but that merely added spice.

"If you're not afraid," he said. "Think of the scandal if the gossip columns got to know about it."

"I can't think of that," she said. "I just want you inside me."

"I never imagined anything like this," Adam said, with a trace of irony.

"It should be like this," she said. "Strange and free like this."

Her fingers wormed inside his tight triangle of silk to touch the rigid flesh. Adam reached down, awkwardly under the water, unzipped the side, kicked the tiny garment off and hung it over one of the iron handgrips. Eve's hand immediately fastened on his organ like a clam. The gentle weight of the sea on his loins accentuated the clean, exhilarating feeling of nakedness and Adam reached down to her loins and slid the tight little bikini over the rotundity of her buttocks so that she could wriggle it down her legs, kick it off her feet, catch it and hang it with his. Adam didn't bother to take off the brassiere. He pushed it up, without undoing it so that her breasts shot out underneath like a nose through a raised vizor.

He could see her lower body floating muzzily white and free below the surface, with the feet kicking gently against the water. Her body was distorted slightly by the sea and he ran his hand down over it to savour its half remembered contours.

"How can we do it?" she asked. "Hurry, I'm dying."

Adam drifted around her, holding her shoulder for support. When he was behind her, with the front of his body pressed against her bare back, he pushed her legs up with his knees so that they formed a horizontal V against the buoy as if she were sitting with her legs apart on the water. Her feet, pressed against the buoy, kept her steady as she held the handgrip with both hands.

Adam reached around her and held the handgrip, too, with each of his hands. And then he let his body float upwards between her legs so that she seemed to be sitting on his lap. The water made him buoyant, held him up against her, and he released the handgrip with his right hand and felt down between her back-sagging buttocks, inching his fingers forward until he found the lips of her vagina, washed strangely dry and cool by the sea. He held his prick and guided it up to these lips. And then as he felt the contact, he pulled her hips down with his one free hand and burst in with a flexing of his hips.

He heard her groan and his penis seemed to him to be quite apart from the cool expanse of the rest of his body which the sea cushioned and washed gently.

His feet, too, found a purchase on the buoy which began to sway ponderously and he began to jerk into her quim with an expert rippling motion of his hips alone.

The water rose and fell around them, but his prick filled her cunt completely and inside there was a soft, clinging warmth which contrasted with the coolness of the rest of their bodies and the chill of the buoy.

Eve began to sag back onto his stiff tower, countering his upthrust and, for brief periods, he found he could let go of the handhold and cling onto her body, grasping the breasts or the belly in luscious handfuls as he shagged her.

He could hear her moaning above the lapping of the waves and the drone of an airplane far above them in the cloudless sky. It was almost as if he were making love to the sea, smooth and voluptuously penetrable and moaning gently under the attack.

"Oh, Adam," she murmured. "It's so good, so wonderful."

He worked his penis higher up into her passage, like a corkscrew in the cork of a wine bottle. His organ was getting hotter and hotter in ever greater contrast to the endless coolness all round them.

He held the handgrip tight and rammed his loins up at the underside of her thighs and buttocks, bringing shrieks from her with every sharp, furious entry. The water around them was churned up a little in a distinct white foam which drifted away from them like scum and gradually disintegrated.

She wriggled her cunt around on the length of his penis, tensing her long, beautiful thighs, gasping out his name. And for seconds at a time he stopped pistoning and just left his bloated, hot, excited cock right up as far as it would go, letting her squirm around on it, bringing pinpricks and waves of shock from it as he contracted his loins.

Adam found that he could lie back in the water, holding onto her breasts, his face just clear of the surface, and let her saw up and down on him, doing all the work and crying with delight at having all the sensation in her own control.

But when he felt the steam rising inside him, bubbling to the boil inside his loins, he clawed up her back again and began to thrust furiously and savagely into her belly, producing a cry of mingled pain and pleasure from her with every brutal stroke.

When she came, the sea went mad around them as if a ship had foundered and wrecked itself and her voice spun across the surface of the bay in a weird siren's cry which broke and sobbed itself into eventual silence.

Adam continued to rub into her with mounting heat and need. His prick was the size of ten and he relied on her completely to keep him up, releasing the handgrip and clasping her belly to pull her hard back onto his staff.

The sensation in his prick grew to the unbearable pressure of a boil being squeezed to bursting point. At the last moment, he thought, this is the great painter screwing the great actress, proving the Colonel's Lady and Judy O'Grady... and then the boil burst with a shattering like the end of the world and his face crumpled and wrinkled in a thousand pressures and his breath was knocked out of him and he fucked his sperm into her quim, pumping it in and in as if from an endless well.

The water held them up and cooled them, helping them to recover with its cleansing, deathless quality.

"As good as a douche," Eve remarked, later, as she wriggled into her bikini.

They began the long swim back to the yacht with lazy, gentle strokes, like a return to a forgotten but unavoidable world.

"Now that we've made up, perhaps we could see more of each other," Eve said.

Adam reflected, his arms slowly cleaving the water like tired oars.

"I dare say," he said... and then more enthusiastically: "We could have a real ball for a weekend once every few months."

"Why so parsimonious with your time?" she asked.

Adam glanced sideways at her as they edged together through the great expanse of the bay.

"You know we can never go back together," he said, "not for a long time anyway."

"Yes," she said thoughtfully. "I do."

"Because," he continued, "we've both got to the crest of the wave by operating like hell... and you have to go on operating to stay there. You'll still have to sleep with people and so will I. There will still be parties and affairs and everything until we decide to call quits and then it won't matter anymore."

"Yes," she said. "It's true. The crest is a lonely place and you can only stay on it by being prepared to sacrifice everything to it. Have we both learned that?"

"We both have, I think," Adam said.

Ahead of them the yacht loomed near and several figures lined the rail to watch them come in. There was no privacy any more.

Adam smiled at her as they swam.

"But we must have plenty of swims in future," he said.

"Yes," she said. "That will be nice. And some day, when I get giddy from being on the crest and you get giddy, maybe we'll meet quietly in the trough—and then we'll have a long, long ball."

THE END